CALIFORNIA ROLL

"Masterful. . . . Observant, wry, wise, funny, vulnerable and tough-minded, Moses Wine has truly come into his own. . . . In *California Roll*, Simon has found an almost perfect voice for [his] character."
—*San Francisco Chronicle*

"Complex . . . entertaining . . . the best Moses Wine mystery Roger Simon has written . . . [he] has created scenes that are not only terrific reading, but make *The Big Chill* appear facile and faked . . . an absolute delight."
—*Los Angeles Herald Examiner*

"Delicious . . . fun!"
—*Newsday*

"Crisp . . . clever—a good entertainment."
—*Houston Chronicle*

"Colorful . . . fun . . . the most entertaining of a cresting wave of suspense novels exploiting the glamour, big money and technological witchcraft of Silicon Valley."
—*San Jose Mercury News*

Also by Roger L. Simon

The Big Fix
Wild Turkey
Peking Duck

Forthcoming from
WARNER BOOKS

CALIFORNIA ROLL

A MOSES WINE DETECTIVE NOVEL

ROGER L. SIMON

WARNER BOOKS

A Warner Communications Company

California Roll is a work of fiction. The characters in it
have been invented by the author. Any resemblance
to people living or dead is purely coincidental.

WARNER BOOKS EDITION

Copyright © 1985 by Roger L. Simon
All rights reserved under International and Pan-American Copyright
Conventions.

This Warner Books Edition is published by arrangement with
Villard Books, a division of Random House, Inc., 201 E. 50 St.,
New York, N.Y. 10022

Cover design by Jackie Merri Meyer
Cover art by Lisa Falkenstern

Warner Books, Inc.
666 Fifth Avenue
New York, N.Y. 10103

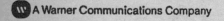 A Warner Communications Company

Printed in the United States of America

First Warner Books Printing: June, 1986

10 9 8 7 6 5 4 3 2 1

For Renée

CALIFORNIA ROLL

1

I NEVER SOLD OUT before because nobody ever asked me. In all it took around twenty minutes. It would have taken around three, but the guy on the other end was so profusely apologetic, he wouldn't give me a chance to say yes.

Actually, if he had any idea of my then depressed state, he might have known that all he had to do was whistle. I was in the midst of a pronounced mid-life crisis somewhere between Gail Sheehy's *Passages* and the advice column of a minor metropolitan daily. I felt like a human cliché. Most of the time I would sit around my room in my bathrobe, listening to Leadbelly albums and bemoaning my situation: three months shy of my fortieth birthday and still a private detective with nothing to show for it but a leaky two-bedroom cottage on Wonderland Drive and a battered Porsche with a severe transmission problem. My political ideals, when I could remember them, felt like the rehash of a twenty-year-old Marcuse paperback. My work, when I had some, was boring. And my body, however hard I fought against it, was beginning its slow, inexorable decay to oblivion.

Beyond this, my kids were growing up and didn't want much more to do with me than an occasional overpriced visit to a sushi bar, while my ex-wife, who had dropped out of law school to live with a movie producer with a ski chalet in Vail and a beach house in Maui, still asked for alimony. And to top it all off, my own lovelife was in the doghouse since the glorious Louise went back to her nitwit stockbroker husband after three years because, after all, she had *her* security to think about. And all around me my sixties buddies were getting rich. "Fuck it, Moses," they would say. "Reagan's in the White House. If you can't lick 'em, join 'em!"

So when the phone call came that Wednesday morning six months ago, I was more than ready, but also a little defensive and maybe a tad paranoid. The guy who was coming to my rescue said his name was Alex Wiznitsky. My first reaction was that it was a put-on. Wiznitsky—or the Wiz, as he is known affectionately—was the cover story of that week's *Time*. WHIZ KID WIZ—IS THE MIRACLE OVER? it said over the determinedly clean-cut face of an aging teenager with shaggy Norman Rockwell hair dripping over his forehead like Beau Bridges. Dozens of unsold computer boxes were stacked behind him to the ceiling of an imaginary warehouse. He wondered if I'd heard of him.

"Sure," I said, suppressing a smile even though we were on the phone. "Sure, I've heard of you."

"Yes, well, I, uh . . . I've heard of you too."

"Good. Then we've both heard of each other." There was a long silence. "What can I do for you?"

"I . . . I know you're going to say no, so I don't know why I'm even b-bothering to ask you but . . . I mean, you'd *never* work for a corporation, would you?"

This time I couldn't suppress a grin. "Well, to be frank with you, I—"

"That's what I thought. I perfectly understand," he interrupted before I could go any further. "Corporations are the instruments of a repressive system whose p-principal goal is the s-sublimation of the individual to collective g-g-greed." He stuttered, too, this Wiznitsky. "I n-never would have w-worked for one either if I hadn't f-founded it myself. I mean, I never even heard of a p-p-public stock offering until two weeks before I made one myself. I mean I'd *heard* of it but . . . "

I presumed he was referring to the stock offering I had read about in that issue of *Time* the previous evening, the one that had netted him $234,000,000 at the age of thirty-one. I didn't realize until later that that $234,000,000 had already dropped to a paltry $116,000,000 because of the downturn in high-tech stocks and the ever-present threat of GTI—General Technology Incorporated—the international behemoth that had insinuated its way into the personal computer market, devouring the competition like so many terrified guppies. But by then I had already undergone a few changes myself—living in a $400,000 Northern California redwood dream house, driving a specially supercharged company-owned BMW 533, going out with a new girl friend who was president of a go-go robotics firm, and visiting a Gestalt therapist *cum* Zen *roshi* to help me adjust to my newfound wealth and status.

The wealth came from the $105,000 a year plus stock options that Wiz offered me, after a lengthy series of stuttering apologies, for becoming the security director of Tulip. The status came from the job itself which, around the Silicon Valley, was, I imagine, like saying you were one of the queen's men at the annual race meeting at Ascot. After all, the valley was where the new legends were being made, and the greatest of those legends was Tulip—a company that had gone from a four-man garage operation behind a Pioneer take-out in Palo Alto to the Fortune 500 inside of three years. And the genius behind it was Wiz—the reluctant debutante who put together the Tulip I and Ii—those nifty little desktop items that revolutionized America even though they were often never used, just left in their boxes in the family den because no one could figure out how to operate the damn things.

The problem was this debutante was *so* reluctant I had to

repeat myself six ways to impress on him that, yes, I did want to take the job.

"Wiz . . . why whould I want to remain a private dick, waiting for the phone to ring from some personal injury attorney who wants me to interview seven witnesses to a fender-bender on the Hollywood Freeway, when I could make my fortune with you in the Silicon Valley?"

"That's what you do? P-personal injuries?" He sounded genuinely surprised, almost hurt.

"Ninety-nine times out of a hundred. The other time is serving processes on widows—ugly ones that spend their days applying Porcelana fade cream."

"But what about the political cases, fighting for the poor, minorities, defending revolutionaries against the c-c-cops?"

"C'mon, Wiz. That all went out with the Buffalo Springfield." But I thought: How would he know? He was about ten at the time.

"You mean you'll take the job?" He sounded almost disappointed.

"When do I start?"

"Anytime. Uh, you can come up t-t-tomorrow, if you want."

"Fine. I just want to warn you. I don't know a thing about computers. I can barely turn on my stereo."

"I need someone with a certain kind of sensitivity for this j-job."

I wasn't sure whether that was supposed to be a compliment. In fact, I wasn't even sure I had the slightest idea what he meant, but I told him I'd be glad to be there anyway.

"Hey, uh, that's t-terrific! I'm just overwhelmed that you're going to do this. I mean, it's a t-total honor."

These computer freaks had a way with words. "I'm pleased too," I said, feeling about forty years older than this guy. "I haven't had any health insurance since college."

"Great . . . uh, Moses?"

"Yes."

"Did you ever see J-Janis Joplin live with the original Big Brother and the Holding Company?"

Oh, Jesus, I thought. What is this guy, a nostalgia buff? I wasn't going to dignify him with an answer, even if he was my new boss.

The Silicon Valley proved to be like the Klondike in the last five years of the Gold Rush. It was as if every two-bit hustler and con artist in the known world had spilled out on that twenty-five-mile strip of industrial parks, shopping centers, and fast-food joints lining Highway 101 between San Jose and Palo Alto, to speculate, wheel and deal, and make a killing before the high-tech mines ran dry. Only this Gold Rush was different, because just when everyone was saying the mines *were* dry, that the rush *was* over, someone invented something new and startling and the game began all over again, on and on until . . . until nobody knew when . . . until the world became bored with video games, laser mirrors, memory circuits, or yet one more featherweight, super-transportable microcomputer to play with in the back seat of the family station wagon.

The day I arrived there I ran straight into a traffic jam as bad as any I had seen in L.A. A thin haze of that familiar yellow stuff hung over the freeway and cars were backed up all the way to Santa Clara. It took us a full forty-five minutes to negotiate the seven-mile drive from the San Jose Airport to Tulip headquarters in Sunnyvale. The "us" in this case was me and my driver—Sharon Kucak—a disappointingly mousy twenty-three-year-old émigré from Haverhill, Massachusetts, who introduced herself as my "area associate." I figured out quickly that that was local parlance for secretary. We crawled along in her Honda Accord—the car of choice, I soon found out, for lower- and mid-level Silicon Valley functionaries—as I answered her obligatory questions about what it was *really like* to be a private eye. Then I listened to her complaints about her boyfriend, an engineer at Hewlett-Packard who was always too busy "nerding out" at his computer to take her to one of the New Wave clubs in San Francisco or even to go for a walk in the redwood groves. We were more than halfway to Sunnyvale before she turned to me with a concerned look on her face.

"You seem like a nice guy, Moses, so I think I better warn you about something." She had an all-purpose ominous dread in her voice that reminded me of my mother. Outside we were passing a granite monolith with the words ADVANCED MICRO DEVICES emblazoned across a space-age porte cochere of Cor-Ten steel. "A lot of people at the company can't figure out why Wiz hired you. I mean, they're pleased to have you and all, but they say you don't know anything about computers and you don't have any experience with technical security systems besides."

"They're right."

"They say Wiz hired you just to get at Witherspoon."

"Who's Witherspoon?"

"The new CEO."

Sharon seemed even more worried when she realized by my expression that I didn't have the slightest idea what a CEO was. She ran her hand in front of her eyes and almost bumped into the Mercedes in front of her. I noticed then that we were swimming in a sea of Mercedes, a higher percentage even than you saw in Malibu or on Rodeo Drive in Beverly Hills.

"The CEO is the chief executive officer of a corporation," Sharon explained to me as if I were the slow child in a remedial reading class. "Mal Witherspoon has just come over to Tulip from the Bellflower Detergent Company, where he was *their* CEO."

"Talk about me. That seems a pretty odd background for a computer company executive."

Sharon looked taken aback. "Mal Witherspoon brought Bellflower Detergent from practically nowhere to number two behind Tide in under a year. Haven't you heard the jingle—'Bellflower makes your dishes the belle of the ball'?" I admitted I'd heard it, ad nauseam, on the radio. "That was his," Sharon continued. "You see, Moses, the valley companies could exist up until a couple of years ago just on their technology, but now we need management, promotion. We have to compete. We can't be just snooty little intellectuals with beepers on our belts. We have to be *real* corporations!"

"You mean it's not what you sell, it's how you sell it."

Sharon looked annoyed with me again. Right then I knew we might have some difficulties, even if she was my "area associate."

"I just wanted to warn you, in case anybody gives you the cold shoulder. Or in case Witherspoon's crowd comes snooping around. They wanted the chief of police from Oakland, who they said had better qualifications." She smiled at me. "But I think you're going to do a great job."

"Thanks," I said as we drove through the gates of the Tulip Computer Corporation—two fifty-foot-high Lucite sculptures shaped in the famous flower logo of the company. Behind it were four large concrete buildings with exposed-steel joists and greenhouse windows resembling giant Tinkertoys. With evident pride Sharon identified them for me—administration, research and development, production, and the then unfinished assembly line for the forthcoming Bulb computer, which would be entirely robotized. Off to the side were the company cafeteria, known for its fresh brioche and Alexander Valley Cabernet Sauvignon, and the "recreational park" with a full-sized gym and jogging track landscaped with native California plants.

"It's like summer camp!" she said.

We parked in a visitor's spot and headed for the administration building. Sharon took the opportunity to point out the Tulip Ethical Code ("the TEC"), which was emblazoned in brass by the front door: THIS CORPORATION BELONGS TO EVERYONE. PRODUCT IS MORE IMPORTANT THAN PROFIT. SERVE THE PUBLIC!

"That was written by the Wiz himself. Back in the garage. . . . It's on every bulletin board!" she enthused, as if these three short sentences were a cross between the Analects of Confucius and the Sermon on the Mount. We turned from the plaque and she opened the door to the building.

"Sounds idealistic."

"Yeah, well, this is a pretty idealistic company. We don't even have time clocks. . . . You know nerds," she added wistfully as she flashed her security badge to a guard. "They like to work between one and four in the morning and then go out for pizza. . . . You have to fill out one of these." She pointed to a temporary pass. I wrote my name next to "Tulip Guest," attached it to my jacket, and followed my "area associate" into the elevator.

Sharon waited discreetly outside the Wiz's office although it was only a doorless "area"—like the other open work spaces on the top floor of the administration building—bounded by cork-lined wallboards and bright-colored Formica paneling in the traditional Tulip colors of peach and lime. I could hear Vivaldi being piped faintly from ceiling speakers as I walked straight in, not knowing if or where I was supposed to knock. The Wiz was sitting at a round oak table in faded jeans and a khaki chamois shirt, watching the Dow Jones averages pass through the terminal of a Ii. If I hadn't known his face from *Time*, I would've assumed he was just another one of the kid programmers on the floor. Standing behind him, pointing at the screen, was a tall, patrician gentleman in a hand-tailored white shirt who reminded me of George Plimpton.

"I told you," said the patrician. "Fifth day in a row—Tulip down four, GTI up three. They've got us dead in the water in six months."

The Wiz shook his head. "We're f-fine."

"Don't be naive." The patrician laughed condescendingly. "We're down forty points."

"That's g-good. We have to go down *and* up. It's the natural en-entropy of the universe. The highest destiny of mathematics is the discovery of order among d-disorder. Only energy is c-constant."

"What?"

"Norbert Wiener—the cy-cybernetician—said that. When he was t-ten years old, he wrote the Theory of Ignorance."

"What has that got to do with the stock market?"

Wiz grinned. "E-everything."

"Sure." The patrician turned away impatiently to see me standing there.

"Moses Wine," I announced. "I have an appointment with the Wiz."

For a second he looked taken aback. "Oh, yes. I'm sorry. Of course . . . our new security director." He extended his hand. "Mal Witherspoon—I'm the ogre from the land of detergents."

"I've heard about you," I said.

"M-M-Moses," said the Wiz, jumping to his feet. "I'm s-so pleased to meet you."

I pumped both their hands.

"You've got some reputation," said Witherspoon. "Unique, unique."

"I'm not sure I know how to take that."

"And I must say you've come in the nick of time. We're in a war here—and we're fighting it on two fronts. You heard about the first one." He nodded toward the computer. "The infamous GTI. But Wiz and I have agreed that you can help us with the other."

He looked over at Wiz, whose mind was elsewhere. "M-M-

Moses, there was something I wanted to ask you on the ph-phone. Have you read the *Zohar*—the p-part that says n-nothing is lost in the world, not even the v-vapor that comes from our mouths?"

"No."

The Wiz looked disappointed. Witherspoon repressed an irritated sigh. "Why don't we fill Moses in on our second front?"

Wiz shook his head distractedly.

"You see the fruits of this man's labor." Witherspoon nodded toward Wiz. "The brilliant inventions he made the last few years are being stolen by everyone in sight—the Japanese, the Koreans, principally the Chinese—and sold for half the price we can sell them."

"Not j-just me. I didn't make those computers alone. They were a—"

"Collective endeavor. Right." The older man rolled his eyes wearily. It was clear that these two had about as much in common as Joan Baez and Nancy Reagan. "Look, the point is—collective or not, the work of this company is being ripped off right and left. We've tried legal means but"—he motioned to a thick stack of briefs—"it's useless. You see, in the Orient, copying someone else's work isn't frowned on. It's an ancient and respected art. They don't have copyright laws and they don't pay attention to ours. With cheap labor they simply take a computer, copy it, and produce it without having to pay a penny of our huge costs in research and development. Not fair, is it?"

I had to agree that it wasn't.

"What we want you to do is stop this."

"Oh," I said, having visions of myself walking into a sweat-shop in Singapore with a sledgehammer and bashing a table full of fledgling computers. It didn't seem like a fruitful assignment.

"Of course, you'll also have the usual administrative problems, overseeing a staff of fifty-two security guards."

Suddenly I was getting a headache.

"Frank Greenwater, director of facilities, will be your immediate superior. He reports directly to me. I realize corporate hierarchies may seem strange to a"—he smiled—"gumshoe. But don't worry. As you might gather, thanks to Wiz, we're pretty loose here at Tulip. Why don't I take you down and introduce you to Frank?"

"N-no," Wiz said suddenly. "L-later. I w-want to talk to Moses alone."

Witherspoon looked at him a moment. "You're the doctor," he said curtly, and turned away. "Nice to meet you." He nodded to me and walked off. I looked over at Wiz, who was already back at his computer, typing intensely. A series of unfathomable equations ran across the screen like rafts down a river.

At length he stopped and motioned toward me. I took a step over as he removed the video terminal and unsnapped the top of the computer. "I-I wanted to show you," he said. "S-so many people are afraid." He pointed inside. "That's the m-mother board and those are the m-microchips. They take the input f-from the k-keyboard and process it. Like a big c-counting house. Over there are the parallel and s-serial ports. They lead to the printer. In-information goes in and out. It's really a very s-simple machine. Very logical and in-innocent. That's why I l-like it." He closed the top and ran his fingers lovingly along the ventilation slats on the side. "It's not like life." His expression became wistful as he looked up at me. "It was such a h-high, Moses, inventing this . . . greater than sex . . . drugs . . . r-religious ecstasy." Suddenly his thirty-one-year-old eyes were as old as the first abacus. "They're t-trying to take the company away from me, Moses."

"I figured."

"Th-they would've already if I h-hadn't started it. Now they'll never be able to. Never." His expression became even sadder. He stroked the computer again, almost as if it were a mechanical security blanket. Then he looked at me once more. "The Orientals are r-right, you know."

"Why?"

"Nothing is an original. Everything is a c-copy."

2

I HAD TO ADMIT I loved it. Working for a corporation was like working for a benign mother who provided everything without making you feel guilty or angry. I loved the office, I loved the expense account. I even loved my "area associate." But most of all I loved not having to worry about myself, loved knowing what I was supposed to do every morning and where I was supposed to be. Even the office gossip was refreshing after twelve years out in the cold.

I spent the first two months familiarizing myself with the job. I took an elementary computer course with a bunch of housewives and CPAs at the local junior college so that I could operate the Tulip Ii the company placed in my redwood living room. Then I gave myself a crash course in computer crime, learning about encryption devices and "data diddling" and "salami attacks"—a subtle ploy by which programmers lopped off small amounts of money (like slices of salami) from the company's computerized accounts until they were ready to take a long vacation in Switzerland. But most of all I studied the "gray market"—that Silicon Valley demimonde where computer chips, often bartered for cocaine and heroin, are sold to jobbers who look the other way and ship them out to the Far East and Europe.

Finally, six months later, I was heading up my first major operation—a "sting" of sorts, designed to trap a powerful Taiwanese computer magnate named Nicky Li, who had been counterfeiting thousands of cheap Tulip computers in Taipei—speeding north on the Bayshore Freeway past Oyster Point in my supercharged BMW. Directly behind me, in a black and white, was Herbert Shear of the DATTA Squad, the new technically oriented subdivision of the San Jose Police Department. To my right, in an unmarked Ford Fairlane, was Barney Harrison, a beefy FBI agent whom, if my memory was correct, I had met about fifteen years before under very different circumstances. I don't think he remembered. We were all headed for the Port of San Francisco to meet the arrival of the SS *Chiang II* from Taipei with a search warrant to examine the shipment of fifteen thousand so-called Chrysanthemum computers to see if they complied with U.S. copyright regulations. Since I had ordered them myself, through a Chinese-American intermediary named Henry Wing, of the newly founded Trans-Pacific Importers, I had every reason to believe they did not. I had further arranged that the producer of these computers, the afore-mentioned Nicky Li, be so pleased with his new San Francisco shipping connection that he would agree to fly in from Taiwan for the arrival of the computers to formalize his relationship with Wing and, of course, to collect his delivery payment of some $2,400,000. I had alerted the media to this very event so that, if all went well, they would be present to photograph Li just as the government seized his counterfeits and he was sent back to Taiwan empty-handed, a grim warn-

brethren that the importation of bogus Tulips
...............owhere near as lucrative as they thought.

This had been the product of four months of careful work
and I was tense as we turned onto 28, heading down toward
the Third Street docks. I had gotten to Li through the theft of
a large batch of semiconductors from a company called Conductel, from which Tulip buys some of its chips. The culprit, a
Chicano junkie named Ortiz who worked in shipping there,
was caught three days later. The chip he had taken—an
EPROM—was one of the keystones in the fabrication of the Ii
and one of the more difficult to copy. In return for leniency, we
got Ortiz to tell the DATTA Squad that he sold them to a place
called Bill's A-1 Wiring in Mountain View.

Now, Bill's was more of a front than any bookie joint I had
ever visited. Herbert Shear and I walked in there one afternoon to get a lamp rewired and they looked at us as if we were
from Mars. A couple of guys were running back and forth
carrying shipping crates to a post office across the street while
someone in the back room was talking long-distance to Taiwan.
That was Bill. He wasn't pleased to see us. But he gave us
Nicky Li's address. He didn't have any choice. And, as luck
would have it, Li had been responsible for more counterfeit
Tulips than any single manufacturer in the last three years.
And now we knew more would be on the way.

So that is how I got involved in this "sting." When I wasn't
walking from building to building making sure someone had
remembered to turn on the card access programs or the corridors were cleared to comply with federal safety regulations, I
worked on it. Witherspoon was pleased to hear about it, though
Wiz, as far as I knew, didn't care. But I had only talked to him
twice in the six months since I'd been hired. He was rumored
to be in seclusion, designing some new super machine. A lot
of people at Tulip were in seclusion, locked up like medieval
monks in the R&D building, working on secret projects no one

could comprehend, hopefully not even GTI, with ironically chosen names like Black Widow and Scalpel.

Nicky Li was not in seclusion. He was to meet Henry Wing at the bar of the Imperial Jade Restaurant on Sacramento Street in Chinatown at 12:30 P.M. There they would sign some documents and then go over to the dock together to inspect the goods.

The Imperial Jade was a run-of-the-mill Cantonese place we had chosen for the poor lighting and the mixed crowd. Shear, Barney Harrison, and I were sitting at a corner table at 12:15, picking at some dim sum. Alice Cantwell, business reporter for the *San Francisco Chronicle*, was at another table with Al Glossbrenner, the stringer for the *New York Times*. At 12:45 Henry Wing walked in. A heavyset former schoolteacher from Fremont, he was dressed in a dark Stanley Blacker business suit we had bought for him for three hundred dollars and carried a Samsonite attaché case. He did not look at us as he sat down at the bar and ordered a glass of beer. I saw the bartender bring over a bottle of Tsingtao. Wing nursed it slowly, glancing at a local Chinese-language newspaper.

Li walked in exactly one minute after the hour. He was a tiny man, almost foppish, in a slate sharkskin suit and purple paisley tie. He looked around the room for a moment, then said a word to the maitre d', who directed him to Wing, seated at the bar. Wing stood and shook his hand. From where I was sitting, Li didn't have the slightest flicker of suspicion. They sat at the bar, where Wing still hadn't finished his beer. Li ordered a Perrier, said a few words in Chinese, and took out a document from a manila folder. Wing glanced at it, nodded. Everything was in order. Li handed Wing a fountain pen to sign what later proved to be a bill of lading. Shear, Barney, and I looked at each other. Everything seemed to be going perfectly. Just then a man burst through the door wearing a navy blue sweater and a body stocking over his head and took three large steps toward Li. Before anybody could move, he had lifted a .357 Magnum, clutching it in both hands, and spattered the Taiwanese all over the bar mirror.

That night I had a date with Sara Blaine, my new girl friend, the president of Toto Robotics ("Toto—the little man that acts like a machine"). I could scarcely call it a heavy date, because these events rarely lasted two hours. That was social life in the Silicon Valley. When it wasn't business oriented, it was something to be squeezed in between a board meeting and an aerobics class. Our dates usually consisted of a quick pita bread sandwich at the local deli followed by about twenty obligatory minutes of clinically orgasmic sex. After that, somewhere around ten, Sara would bounce out of bed and—all full of excuses how, in the robot business, if you weren't moving ahead you were falling behind—head back to her office to dictate memos.

But not that night. That night she wanted to go through the whole *Kama Sutra* with several chapters of the *Book of Tantra* thrown in for dessert. When I was thoroughly spent, rolling over on the mattress like a whipped dog, she still looked at me as if she had somehow fallen into bed with a combination of Sean Connery and Mr. T.

"So they wrapped him up in a body bag and everything?"

"Uh-huh. That's what they do," I said, reaching for the bottle of nearly flat Heineken on the headboard.

"Wow. You live an exciting life. Who do you think did it? Terrorists?"

"Haven't the foggiest."

"Well, what about the computers?"

"They're in the hands of the Customs Service."

"What're they going to do with them?"

"Not much. They don't work."

Sara sat up straight and shivered, shaking her tumbling mane of blonde hair which always reminded me of a Clairol advertisement. Then she looked at me intently, hanging on every word. I had to admit I was enjoying this.

"The EPROM chips were removed," I explained.

"Who's got them?"

"No one in this country. It's not likely they even made it onto the boat."

"They'll probably show up in somebody else's counterfeit Tulips," she said gravely, playing the detective.

I shrugged, feigning worldliness. The truth was that the event *did* have me baffled. I had unleashed forces I had in no way foreseen and without the slightest clue to their source. It might have been the result of some ancient tong war for all I knew. Indeed, that is the way the local papers played it up the next morning. COMPUTER WARLORDS! screamed the *Examiner*. I had my doubts. Whatever it was, it had turned a devoted workaholic into a torrid sensualist. Before I knew it, Sara was reaching for my crotch and guiding me under the covers again.

"Don't you have a sales conference tomorrow morning?" I couldn't resist the dig.

"Shithead!" she said, jumping out of bed. "You know how to ruin everything." She grabbed her pants and started pulling them on. "No wonder you've been alone half your life."

It wasn't exactly half, but it hardly seemed worth contradicting her. "Truce," I said.

"Too late. Toto's more interesting than you are. He makes my coffee, he's user-programmable, and he isn't a snide sonofabitch."

"Well, this is the first time I've lost out to a robot." I took a swig of the Heineken. "But I suppose that's the wave of the future." I gave her my most sincere, self-pitying puppy dog look. For a moment it seemed like it was going to work when there was a buzz from my computer.

"It's your modem." Sara pointed at the signal light blinking from the small communications module above my terminal. "Maybe it's one of those obscene computer dating services you like so much."

I turned away. Actually, the night before, I had been on-line with a woman from St. Louis who wanted to do things to my prostate gland I had never dreamed existed. "Aren't you going to log-on?" said Sara, sensing my hesitation.

I walked over to the computer, pressed A, and connected. The buzzer went off again and the following appeared immediately on the video terminal:

```
Welcome, Moses. Do you want to retrieve
your messages now? Y/N
```

I pressed Y. The screen wiped to reveal:

```
Message #1, 9:45:42, Logic and knowledge
are not the same. Men will try to kill
you and the Black Widow will die. If you
wish to survive, use your artificial
intelligence.
                              Cassiopeia
```

"Cassiopeia? Who the fuck is Cassiopeia?"

"The mother of Andromeda," said Sara. I was impressed. "Andromeda married Perseus, who rescued her from a sea monster. . . . Moses." She touched my shoulder. "What's going on? Is somebody trying to kill you?"

"Not as far as I know." I grinned. "Want to get Toto to guard me?"

"Don't be funny. This is serious. . . . Maybe I should stay here tonight."

"Maybe you should," I said. Somehow I wasn't taking this death threat seriously. But I didn't know why not. Twelve hours before, I had seen a Taiwanese industrialist's cerebellum turned into chopped brie.

Sara stayed, but I wasn't sure how I felt about this being the instigation of our first full night together. When she got up, she was in a testy mood and left quickly because her morning rituals had been disrupted. There was no *Wall Street Journal* at my door and she didn't have her vitamins. Sara was a typical creature of her time and took a raft of vitamins with every meal. She also exercised rigorously, spending up to two hours a day on Nautilus machines, treadmills, bikes, and something called a Hydra-Gym that poured enough water into a weight-lifting cylinder to break the back of a large Swedish lumberjack.

All this sweat and vigor shamed me into doing some of it myself and I had started 'taking an evening turn on the company jogging track. Soon I was up to four miles a day plus three visits a week to the weight room, tugging away at a Universal machine and discovering muscles I thought had gone into permanent hibernation at the age of nineteen. It was that following afternoon, huffing and puffing my way between the native-grown ceanothus, that I ran into Witherspoon in the peach-and-lime Tulip jogging suit made for the company store by the Adidas Corporation. He signaled me to join him. Witherspoon was a lean and experienced corporate jogger from the roof of the New York Athletic Club and he kept a good pace as we strode past the back of the gym. I matched him stride for stride, trying not to breathe too heavily and reveal that I was having trouble keeping up with this man who was ten years older than me.

"Keeping fit, I see," he said at length. "We're considering putting in a parcourse. What do you think?"

"Good idea," I grunted.

"You know, Moses—this Nicky Li affair. We have to be careful. It's a nasty business." He kicked up the pace and I struggled to stay with him. "I know you were a crack private investigator and everything but you're working for a corporation now and sometimes it's better just to keep a low profile, if you know what I mean."

"Don't worry. We don't have a choice. The feds are in it and they don't want any private parties lurking about."

"Just as well." We reached the end of the course and he stopped at the base of a brittlebush, genus *Encelia*. (All the plants along the track were labeled with redwood plaques giving their common and Latin names.) "You should concentrate on Danny Rigrod."

"Danny Rigrod?"

"Chief engineer for the Black Widow project. He's kind of a weirdo. They call him the Last Nerd."

The Last Nerd. I smiled to myself. It was amazing. The nerds had had their day and it had lasted for just five years— five years in the sunlight for all those horn-rimmed high school outcasts who hid in the family basement playing with wires and doing equations while the rest of us were out trying to get laid or wrecking the family car—and now it was over. They were back as outcasts again, at least semi-outcasts, pushed firmly out of the limelight and into their laboratories again by Witherspoon and the rest of the satraps of the bottom line.

"What's wrong with Rigrod?" I asked him.

Witherspoon stooped to drink from the spring-water fountain. "He's been missing for a week."

"Maybe he just skipped out and is taking an unplanned vacation someplace. You know Tulip—no time clocks, no structures."

"His roommate says there's not a stitch of clothing missing. Even his toothbrush is still in the cup in the medicine cabinet."

"That's what I mean. Nerds like to travel light." I smiled. I couldn't resist having fun with Witherspoon. "They like to go up in the High Sierras with just their radio telescopes and listen for alien intelligence."

Witherspoon smirked.

"Who's his roommate?"

"A nerd named Alf Richardson."

"Another nerd? I thought Rigrod was the last one."

"Very funny, Moses." He wasn't amused. "They share an old Spanish house up in Los Gatos. Rigrod made a lot of money in software before he came to work for Tulip. They say he's some kind of genius. Graduated first in his class from MIT when he was only nineteen."

"I'll go talk to Alf."

"Fine . . . but do this one quietly, please. Black Widow is an important project, and if he's off selling trade secrets to GTI, we don't want the public to know about it."

I nodded. "By the way—what is the Black Widow?"

"I wouldn't know. And needless to say, if I did, I wouldn't understand it." Witherspoon smiled thinly, pulled on the hood of his jogging suit, and walked off.

Sara was demonstrating Toto at a trade fair in Anaheim, so after I showered and ate, I drove up Highway 85 to Los Gatos to have a talk with Alf Richardson. Within five minutes I had left the suburban dullness of the valley floor and was winding through the Santa Cruz Mountains past eucalyptus groves and twisted live oaks flourishing in the bottoms of dry riverbeds. A brilliant orange sun was setting off to my left, making the whole scene a postcard California dream. This was where many of the winners in the Silicon Valley rat race got to enjoy the spoils of their victory. Some of them never even came out of their homes, a new generation of computer commuters connected through modems to their home bases in the industrial parks below.

Rigrod and Richardson lived still farther out, in the back country of Los Gatos, and it wasn't until I turned off 85 onto a twisting two-lane road called Rinconada Way that I began to suspect I was being followed. By this time the sun had set and I could see the headlights of the other vehicle glinting through the foliage as I veered back and forth. I slowed to check my suspicion of a brown Ford Grenada with California plates. Then I sped up again and roared around the corner. But my companion was not interested in playing games and turned around at the next driveway.

I arrived at my destination five minutes later—a quarter-mile private road leading to a gorgeous Monterey-style rancho perched on the side of the mountain. It looked unoccupied as I walked toward the front door, taking in the panoramic view of the valley lights in one direction and the moonlit Pacific in the other. A large redwood deck stretched off to the side of the building with what looked like a newly built pool and hot tub. The open three-car garage was fully stocked with a Mercedes turbo-diesel, a black Jeep, and a silver Porsche 928, a good eighty grand in automotive equipment. Peeking out behind that was a greenhouse where I recognized the outline of a familiar psycho-active plant growing under small nocturnal spotlights.

"Need help?"

I turned to see a tall, ungainly young man in his mid-twenties wearing a down vest and a watch cap. He was holding a frisky little black and white goat tightly on a leash by his side.

"I'm looking for a man named Alf Richardson."

"I'm Richardson," he said.

"I'm Moses Wine." I nodded toward the house. "May I come in?"

Richardson tightened. "You better tell me who you are first."

"I work for Tulip. I'm the security director."

"Oh, I heard about you." He studied me carefully for a moment. "This must be about Danny." He nodded toward the goat. "Let me tie up Turing first or he'll devour everything in sight."

"Turing? As in Alan Turing?"

"You know about him?"

"Not much," I said as Richardson tied the goat to a post. "He was the English computer genius who broke the Nazi code during the war. And he killed himself, didn't he? When they discovered he was a homosexual."

Richardson nodded almost imperceptibly. He walked over and opened the door of the house.

Inside it was like a college dormitory for the richest pair of undergraduates I had ever seen. All of the furniture was new, some of it with the shipping box, still intact, sitting next to it. Books, records, magazines, sweaters, underwear, and floppy disks were strewn everywhere at random. There were video tape decks and computers in every room, but most of them didn't seem to be hooked up or had wires sticking out of the terminals like cowlicks. Over the mantelpiece was a huge blowup of Richardson at about the age of thirteen with another boy I took to be Rigrod. Both of them were dressed in dark blue suits with dopey grins on their faces in the dumb, posed style of a bad bar mitzvah photo.

"I take it you've known Danny a long time."

"Since we were seven years old. We grew up together in Winnetka, Illinois. He was my only friend. You know what it was like in high school. People thought guys like us had warts coming out of our ears. We got 'em, though." He smiled briefly, gesticulating at the house. "Made a million in data base management. And the president of our high school class—you know what happened to him?" Richardson pulled a joint from his shirt pocket. "Had a little liquor store right on Stevenson Street, where we all grew up. Went bankrupt and now he's in the state mental hospital for chronic alcoholism." He lit the joint. "Want some?" I had a hit, just to be polite. "Don't worry about Danny," he said. "He's fine."

"How do you know?"

"I talked to him a few days ago."

"Where was he?"

"He didn't say. . . . Hey, look, don't worry about it. I *know* Danny." He laughed softly. "If I thought something was wrong, I'd've called the police. He said he's doing something important and when it's over, he'll be back."

"Don't move," I said. He looked at me peculiarly. "Stay exactly where you are and keep talking to me as if I were still here."

Richardson looked blank. For someone who could design advanced programs in data base management he was a little slow on the uptake. "Oh, yeah," he said finally. "Okay."

He started moving his lips as I backed slowly out of the sight line of his living room window, almost knocking over a stack of old technical journals and a plate of moldy Hostess cupcakes on the floor behind me that looked like they had been there since the early Pleistocene Age.

I found a side door and quietly slipped the lock, sliding outside into the moonlight. From that angle I could see Turing tethered to the post and the Ford Grenada parked way up at the top of the private road. The figure of a barrel-chested man was silhouetted against a pepper tree, watching a tense Richardson mouthing unintelligible syllables to an imaginary respondent. I drew closer to him, then decided to have a look at the car. Keeping one eye peeled back on the barrel-chested man, I crept up the grassy shoulder of the private road toward the Grenada. I drew just close enough to read the license plate when I heard someone cry out "Victor!" I turned as a fist the size of a Smithfield ham came hurtling toward me like a meteor in free fall. It was lights out from there on in.

3

I WOKE UP LATE the next morning feeling like a blind coyote who had just been run over by a semi. My jaw was distended and there was a thin strip of gauze wrapped around my forehead which, in the mirror, made me look like a World War I victim on the way back from the front. I peeled it off gingerly, still wondering at the flat expression on Richardson's face the previous night as he drove me to Emergency at the Santa Clara Valley Hospital. Despite what had occurred, he was still certain nothing had happened to his friend.

I cleaned up the wound with some hydrogen peroxide and redressed it before Sharon—all solicitousness over my injury—picked me up and drove me by Richardson's for my car. The engineer wasn't there, so I continued on to my office to check on the plates of the Ford Grenada. It was rented from a Hertz dealership in San Francisco by one P. J. Evans with what proved to be a phony New Jersey driver's license. No "Victor" there. My head was still throbbing and Sharon made me some black coffee, which I swallowed with one of the Empirin-codeine compounds they had given me at the hospital. Then I pushed some paper around and waited for the anesthesia to set in. When I felt better, I decided to pay a visit to the offices of the Black Widow project.

The offices were on the fourth floor of R&D, the high-security research building at Tulip. To get in you needed an access card similar to those plastic jobs replacing keys at the fancier hotels. And even once you were inside your movements were restricted. The same access card that let you in controlled the elevator, but it was programmed only to let you out at the floor where you were working. The card also admitted you to your office or laboratory, but only *when* you were supposed to be there, all the while recording your arrivals and departures in the master computer. Some key personnel were allowed cards that accessed their own offices at any time, but only five people had cards that gave them unrestricted movement in the building—Witherspoon, the Wiz (who never came around), Frank Greenwater (as director of facilities), Sheldon Margolis (as director of R&D), and me (as security director). The system seemed rather elaborate, but on closer inspection was totally absurd. Given the minds of the people who worked in the building, any of them could have cracked it in a matter of minutes while eating their lunch and talking on the telephone at the same time. But, as Frank Greenwater explained to me when he introduced me to the system, it created a certain "moral suasion," whatever that meant, not to mention a general atmosphere of "security consciousness." He chose to ignore me when I asked him if that had anything to do with the Tulip Ethical Code.

The fourth floor itself was known as Nerd Central around the company because it had the reputation of housing the farthest-out projects. It seemed appropriate that the Last Nerd worked there, at least when he showed up. The Black Widow offices were at the end of the corridor past Scalpel and Jujube—two projects working in VLSI, or Very Large Scale Integration chips. I walked quickly past them and knocked on the door of Black Widow. It was opened by a tall, broad-shouldered blond man in a blue workshirt and horn-rimmed glasses who looked something like a Nordic Clark Kent. He had a pencil behind each ear and his eyes were half buried in *Barron's Business Weekly*.

"Nobody's here right now," he mumbled, scarcely looking up from the magazine.

"My name's Moses Wine. I'm the security director. It's about Danny Rigrod."

"Oh, the prodigal son." He backed up, allowing me to enter.

The offices of Black Widow were anything but prepossessing—just a couple of austere rooms with a desktop computer in each and some long tables stacked with plans. I noticed a paper shredder under one of them.

"I'm Eddie Capshaw," my host told me, extending his hand and shaking mine firmly. For a bespectacled engineer, this man had a grip like a construction worker. "I'm staff logician," he continued. "There's only three of us. Black Widow isn't a very big operation."

"Just what is Black Widow anyway?"

"Well, it's kind of hard to explain. Do you know how to program in PROLOG or LISP?"

"No . . . but I know a little BASIC."

"Yeah . . . uh-huh." He looked at me as if he had just asked if I was fluent in Serbo-Croatian and I had replied no, but I knew a little Pig Latin. He sighed and continued patiently. "What we're working on is heuristic programming . . . expert systems." This didn't ring a bell either. "Hey, it's like you're a detective, right? And you put everything you know into the computer—how to follow people, how to find missing children, how to pick up blondes." He grinned. "Then someone wants to solve a case—they press a button. That's an expert system!"

"And what kinds of experts does Black Widow deal with?"

"Ah, that's very complicated. This is experts on experts on experts. No one knows all of it. Not even Danny. Hey . . ." He held up *Barron's*. "What do you think of Intertel at thirty-five? Guy in here says it's a good bet to split three-for-one in six months."

"I wouldn't know." I shook my head. Everyone in this town was out to make a killing. Soon they'd be passing out stock tips with the Green Stamps at supermarkets. "You have any idea where Danny might be?"

He shrugged. "Haven't seen him in a week, like everybody else . . . but if I were looking, I'd try the Rainbow."

"The Rainbow?"

"Tacky, huh?"

He was right. The Rainbow was pretty well known in Silicon Valley, a seedy topless bar over in Sunnyvale where uptight engineers from nearby companies ogled tired strippers who looked like refugees from a local cellulite clinic. But it was said you could learn more about the latest high-tech trends while guzzling the watered-down drinks at the Rainbow than from all the technical journals in America combined. Deals were made at the Rainbow, employees were raided, and more than a few secrets stolen.

"He hangs out there a lot?"

"Not until the last couple of months. He was too shy, even to watch girls at a bar. But somewhere around the middle of September, he started to go every day."

"How do you know?"

"I went with him a couple of times. He wanted me to meet this friend of his. One of the strippers."

"Who was that?"

"Her name was Paula. That's what he called her, anyway. But I don't think that was her real name."

"What was her real name?"

"I don't know. I only met her once. She had an accent . . . Polish, I think. At least she danced in a Solidarity T-shirt."

"A Solidarity T-shirt?"

Capshaw nodded. "With a G-string."

I had to smile. The image of some overweight Polish fräulein sashaying along a runway to bad disco music while a bunch of engineers stuffed dollar bills in her G-string for the greater glory of Lech Walesa was a treat I didn't want to miss.

"Does she do this every night?"

"No. At lunch." He pointed to his watch. "In around ten minutes."

I nodded. "Thanks for the help."

"Yeah." He smiled. "See you around, Spade."

The lot of the Rainbow was two-thirds empty when I arrived at 12:25 that afternoon. I found a spot near the door and walked straight in. Inside, the place had the look of a second-rate Tijuana nightclub that was about to go out of business: a dimly lit bar and tables with a few Day-Glo animal paintings interspersed with some dog-eared Playmates of the Month circa 1977. But no Paula. Instead, a stripper who looked Chicana was doing a pitiful imitation of a bump-and-grind on the runway to a monotonous Styx album. She wasn't topless at all but wore a full one-piece leopard-skin body leotard that did little to disguise the bulges about her midsection. At this hour the guys around her didn't look much like engineers either, but more like shippers and handlers, unemployed or on long lunch hours. I recognized one of them from the Bulb plant and he gave me the eye, probably wondering if I had come to turn him in for malingering or for selling "jelly beans"—cheap, outdated chips—to the guy on the next stool.

I was about to take a place at the bar when I noticed a Japanese girl of about twenty-five leaning against a pinball machine in the corner. She was startlingly beautiful, with a pale, porcelain complexion and jet-black hair that shot over her shoulders in quick jagged slashes like the strokes of a brush painting.

I wandered over and leaned against the opposite wall, studying her. Her eyes were as black as her hair, and despite her tattered jeans and pale gray T-shirt, she had a haughty bearing, almost aristocratic, that made it hard to believe she was a stripper.

"What's your name?" I asked.

"Laura." The word was barely audible.

"How about some doubles?" I nodded toward the pinball machine and took out a couple of quarters. "My treat."

She didn't answer but just surveyed me with the coldest look imaginable this side of Lapland. Then, with half a wave worthy of a shogun's geisha, she turned away, dismissing me as if I were some pathetic feudal peasant who had the temerity to beg for alms at her lord's palace. I slumped away, feeling about six inches off the ground and shrinking.

I managed to pull myself up on the bar stool and order up a draft Michelob. I surveyed the scene awhile, watching the action, what there was of it. The waitresses were mostly surly and bored. From the way he guarded the cash register, the pot-bellied man seated at the end of the bar was obviously the owner. I finished off my Michelob and sidled down to him. He was browsing through his accounts and didn't notice me as I came up.

"Hi," I said.

"Hello," he returned unenthusiastically. Behind his head were signed photos of engineers. One read:

TO AL
YOU MAKE MY DAY!
PHIL OF SIGNETICS

"I'm looking for Paula." I took it as casually as possible. "She been around?"

"Who?"

"Paula . . . you know . . . I'm a friend of hers from a long time back."

"I don't know any Paula." He still didn't look up from his books.

"That's funny," I said. "She said she worked here."

"She did?" More unenthusiasm.

"The Polish girl from Solidarity."

Al's eyes lifted from the page like a turtle coming out of its shell for the first time in a week, carefully and very slowly. He studied me with a leaden expression before speaking. "Her name's not Paula," he said finally.

"Oh, yeah. I know that," I said, giving it another few seconds. "What's she call herself around here?"

"What's she call herself where you come from?"

"Hilda," I said. "Hilda Cybulski."

"Good." He returned to his books.

I leaned in closer and whispered. "It's about her brother in Krakow. They won't let him out, but we have some news."

"Oh, yeah? Who're you?" He looked at me pointedly.

"A sympathetic friend of the family. I want to help Hilda. I'm sure you want to help her too."

"Uh-huh."

"It makes me cry to think her family will spend the rest of their lives living in tyranny." I stared at the owner. I couldn't tell if I was making any progress, but I continued anyway. "After a while you get to feel responsible. Somebody's got to take a stand, don't you agree?" I leaned in closer. "Even Reagan took the risk of blowing our relations with China by letting that little tennis player defect . . . remember?"

"Oh, Jesus, a goddamn Eagle Scout. What're you—a member of the John Birch Society?"

"Just a concerned citizen."

Al let out a deep sigh. "A concerned citizen, huh? All right. But don't say you heard it from me. Anna's the girl you're looking for. Anna Wajda." He started going through his books. "She hasn't been around here for a while. She never had a phone but the last address I have for her is 23 Guadalupe Avenue in San Jose." I was about to thank him when my beeper went off. Everyone around me started staring. "Whatsa matter?" said Al, smiling superciliously. "You wanted in surgery?"

I grunted and went off to a pay phone. My eyes were on the Japanese girl again as I dialed Sharon. But I turned away and cupped the phone when I heard the news: The police had just pulled the corpse of Danny Rigrod out of a dry river wash a quarter-mile west of the Lexington Reservoir near Los Gatos. He had been shot in the face at point-blank range by a .357 Magnum. Ballistics experts were checking to see if it was the same one that had decimated Nicky Li. By the time I got to the morgue, they had decided that it wasn't.

4

THAT NIGHT I SPENT about forty-five minutes on the phone with Witherspoon promising him I wouldn't talk to the press. He wasn't easy to convince.

"Private detectives are all hungry for publicity," he said. "It's your life blood."

"I'm not a private detective anymore. I work for Tulip."

"You were on the cover of *Rolling Stone*."

"That was nine years ago, for crissakes. It was a different era. Even though my hair never came below my ears, they thought a hippy private eye made good copy."

"Well, this is Silicon Valley 1984 . . . Poles . . . Solidarity . . . mysterious research. Think of the copy that makes!"

"Witherspoon . . . really. . . . You think some reporter at the *Chronicle*'s gonna top your salary for a thirty-minute interview and cappuccino at Enrico's?"

An operator broke onto the line. "555-1964, you have an emergency call from Jacob Wine in Los Angeles. Do you wish to accept?"

"Sure," I blurted. "Sorry, Witherspoon," I added, trying to disguise the glee in my voice. I hung up before he could protest. The phone rang a few seconds later. I picked up quickly. I hadn't spoken to him in about a week and I was feeling a little guilty.

"Hello."

"Hello, Dad." He sounded depressed.

"What's up?"

"Guess what?"

"You got another C in trig. Don't worry about it. It's a family tradition. You'll make it up in bullshit courses like government and art history."

"I had an accident."

My heart sank somewhere between my kneecap and my big toe. Jacob had gotten his license three weeks ago and was the proud owner of a '67 Renault willed to him by my ex-wife's parents. To the relief of an anxious father, it was the kind of car that could barely make it from zero to sixty in fifteen minutes—and then it had to be jump-started and pointed downhill with everybody in the front seat, leaning forward.

"Are you all right?"

"Yeah, yeah. Nobody was hurt. It's just the Renault. It kinda got some heavy damage."

"How heavy?"

"Seven hundred bucks."

I took a deep breath.

"I lost my job at the croissant place last week and I thought—you're making good money now and maybe you could help me out."

"What about your mother? She's as rich as Rose Kennedy these days."

"She's off in Maui with Jay."

Jay, I thought. Everybody in Hollywood was named Jay. Jay or Sidney.

"What about Simon?" I asked, suddenly alarmed.

"Don't worry. He's with her."

"And you?"

"I'm staying with Julie."

"Who's Julie?"

"This girl. But don't worry—her parents are Mormons and they make us sleep in opposite wings of the house. It's got seven bedrooms."

"Who's worrying?" There was a knock on my door. "Just a second."

I went to open it to reveal a three-foot-high robot standing on my doorstep. In a moment, it started to beep and wobble into the room. I rushed back to the phone.

"Jacob, I've got a visitor. I'll send you some money for the car. When you get it fixed, maybe you and, uh, Julie can drive up and visit me."

I hung up just as the robot was about to crash into a lamp. I grabbed the lamp away and the robot bumped into my toe, heading off in the opposite direction, barely missing upending the potted cactus by the television.

"I am Toto, your servant," it said to me in a growly voice resembling someone scratching on the inside of a washtub as it beeped and wobbled into the kitchen. "Tell me what you want."

"For starters, I want you to stay out of the refrigerator."

"Toto will stay out of the refrigerator." It gurgled and whirred with a noise I supposed was putting that information into its permanent program. "Tell me what you want."

It stood there awaiting my instructions. For the first time I took a good look at the mechanical creature. It had a single crablike pincer for an arm, rollers for legs, and two huge glass eyes, one on top of the other, that made it look something like a moving streetlamp.

"Go on, tell it." It was Sara's voice. I turned to see her standing in the kitchen doorway with a wide grin on her face. "He's yours now. Fourth one off the assembly line. . . . I heard about Danny Rigrod and I thought you might need someone around."

"Ah, protection. . . . Toto, let's see your ray gun."

"Toto does not have a ray gun. Tell me what you want."

"No ray gun? What good are you for protection? Do you have a piece?"

"Toto does not understand 'piece.' Tell me what you want."

"How about a martini?"

Toto started to whir and gurgle again. "What part gin? What part vermouth?"

"Hey, not bad!" I said to Sara. "Scratch the martini, Toto. We're out of vermouth."

"Toto does not understand 'scratch the martini.' Tell me what you want."

"All right. All right." I turned back to Sara. "He's as bad as a shrink—always asking me what I want all the time."

Sara nodded. "Toto's very direct. Like all expert programs nowadays—straight and uncomplicated. But he's programmed only to listen to you. Who else can you say that about? Tell him to go on alert mode."

I turned to the robot. "Toto, on alert mode."

The robot did an immediate about-face and headed back into the living room, this time crashing straight into the cactus, upending the entire plant, and scattering pebbles all over the living room floor. This didn't deter the robot, however, which continued straight on to the front door, standing there proudly, facing outward with its claw in the air. "Toto on alert!" it said, its lights flashing on and off like beacons at an airport.

"Should sell a lot at Christmas," I said. "Especially to people who don't like plants."

"I'm sorry, Moses," said Sara. "He is only the fourth one, though. Be easy on him."

"Oh, sure," I said.

She reached into the kitchen closet and pulled out the dust pan and broom, returning to the living room to deal with the cactus pebbles. "So what's with Danny Rigrod? What's your next move?" she asked, sweeping them in while I held the pan.

"I'm not sure," I said. "The cops said the Polish girl checked out of the place on Guadalupe, but I thought I'd have a look for myself tonight."

"Can I come along?" she said. "We can leave Toto on guard."

"You mean you don't have to prepare for tomorrow's board meeting?" Again I couldn't resist a little dig.

"Moses." She gave me a sour look. Why was it I was always attracted to women who were powerful and interesting in their own right, yet I had this compulsion to pick a fight with them at the same time, maybe even wreck the relationship? I made a note to ask my shrink when he got back from vacation.

Something similar must've been on Sara's mind as we drove over to San Jose. "Do you think what Woody Allen said is true?" she asked.

"What's that?"

"That a relationship is like a shark—either it moves forward or it dies."

I shrugged. It was a hard prescription. Where did that leave my aunt Ethel and uncle Mike, who were married to each other for sixty years? The only thing sharklike about them was all the corned beef sandwiches they ate. Maybe it was just my generation, all us narcissists who wanted so much fulfillment from one another that no one could provide it for more than a month.

I could sense that Sara and I were both mulling over similar matters as we pulled into the place on Guadalupe Avenue. It was in a lower-middle-class residential area, dark and tree-lined, and the image of a .357 Magnum suddenly flashed into my brain. I felt apprehensive and more than a little unprofessional about having taken Sara along. But leaving her in the car at this point seemed equally dangerous, so I nodded for her to follow me to the apartment building.

It was a temporary residence hotel with the unlikely name of Redwood Mansions, although it was constructed entirely of stucco in the style I liked to call California–Middle East, built to fall apart before it was even finished. Anna Wajda's name was still listed under apartment 3E and I made a note of it as Sara and I walked down to the manager's door and rang the bell. An unshaven man in his sixties opened the door wearing a ratty bathrobe and slippers. His breath smelled like a cross between halitosis and cheap muscatel.

"Hello," I said. "My name's Litvak. I'm looking for a small apartment."

He looked over at Sara, who was extremely well dressed in a pant suit by some fancy Italian designer. "For the hour, for the week, for the year . . . what?"

"We're here on business. Maybe a couple of weeks."

"2B's open. Cost you two hundred in advance with another fifty breakage deposit." He looked at me suspiciously. "That your BMW parked outside?"

"Oh, that—just a rental." I forced a laugh. "You know, sometimes you gotta treat yourself. Besides, if you don't think rich, you never get rich—know what I mean?" He didn't react. "Look, I don't think 2B will work out. She's kinda superstitious." I nodded toward Sara. "She was in Vegas once when the hotel burned down and she was on the second floor at the time."

"I barely escaped with my life," added Sara.

"Got anything on, say, the third floor?" I asked.

The manager swallowed, suppressing a burp. "Yeah, well, something just opened up . . . but I'm not sure I'm supposed to rent it right away."

"Why not?"

"I dunno. A police matter."

"Jesus!" I looked outraged. "Government intervention. No wonder we're falling behind the Japanese. There's so much goddamn red tape around here you can't make a living. Well, there's always the Holiday Inn. C'mon, sweetheart."

I took Sara's arm and we started out.

"What a minute!"

A few seconds later the manager was opening the door of 3E, but he didn't look very happy about it. He followed us into the apartment, a spartan one-bedroom affair with a peeling linoleum-tiled kitchen and shoddy Naugahyde furniture. I peered into the bathroom and the closet. Everything had been cleaned out.

"Who lived in here . . . a monk?"

"Goddamn Polack broad."

"What's wrong with them? You don't like their jokes?" He didn't answer. I switched on the floor lamp but it wouldn't work. "Something the matter with your electrical system?" I asked.

"No way, mister. I changed all the bulbs yesterday. This place is perfect. It's got air conditioning, gravity heating . . . next month we might even put in microwaves."

"Changed the bulb, huh?" I said, frowning as I studied the lamp. "Mind if I have a look at it? I'm kinda handy with these things."

Sara gave me a strange look as I kneeled down and started to examine the socket.

"Hey, what're ya doin'?" said the manager. He took a threatening step toward me.

"Must be a problem with the wiring," I said. Before the

manager could reply, I pulled out the plug. As I had expected, it felt peculiarly hollow. I tugged at the plastic cover and the plate came off immediately. "Boy, you guys better do something about your electrical system. This thing doesn't even look up to code." I carefully reached in, not surprised to find that the entire junction box had been removed. A couple of scraps of paper were inside and I palmed them carefully while replacing the cover. Then I stood and made a show of surveying the room. "I'll have to think about it," I said, facing the manager, who now looked very worried. "We've got one of those elaborate stereo outfits and it might overload the whole building. Thanks for the look around, though."

I led a puzzled Sara out of the place as rapidly as possible.

"The Polish girl was hiding her information in the electric socket," I told her, hurrying down the stairs. "I knew a dealer who did the same thing with his stash. Not a bad place if you don't want prying hands fiddling around with your coke."

We exited the building and crossed quickly to my car. I could see the manager staring at us through the window as I drove off. Two blocks later I pulled over and took the scraps of paper out of my jacket pocket and unfolded them. The larger proved to be a Xerox of a National Car Rental map of the Silicon Valley. The other was a telephone number beside some words in a scrawled script I took to be Polish. I stopped at the nearest phone booth and dialed the number. It had been disconnected.

The next morning I had the Polish translated by an import-export service in San Francisco:

He says he has a *Mania for Death*. Project Blowfish is almost finished. 555-7234.

Mania for Death. Project Blowfish. It made no sense to me. Witherspoon had no idea what it meant either, and I put a call through to the Wiz, but he was in seclusion, not to be disturbed. I left a message with his area associate that it was urgent and then went off to pay another visit to the Black Widow offices.

This time when the door opened I had to fight hard to keep my jaw from dropping to the floor. Instead of Capshaw, I was greeted by the same elusive Japanese girl who had been standing by the pinball machine at the Rainbow the previous day. I could see by her expression that she was equally surprised to see me.

"Hello, Laura."

"Oh, hi. You're the guy from the bar."

"That's right. My name's Moses Wine."

"Oh, my God, the security director." She looked embarrassed. "You must've thought I was a real snob. I'm sorry. I'd never been to that place before and I didn't know what to expect. It has this reputation, you know."

"What were you doing there?"

"Same thing you were, I suppose. Looking for Danny. It's such a tragedy what happened. I was up all night crying. Who do you think did it?"

I followed her into the office. "I don't know much. He seems to have been palling around with a Polish friend."

"So I've heard." She turned and tried to smile at me. She was wearing another pair of jeans and a tight-fitting T-shirt with an old Japanese print silk-screened on the front. The best of East and West. "Oh," she said, extending her hand. "I haven't introduced myself. I'm Laura Suzuki—a programmer for Black Widow."

"Been working here long?"

"Two years. Since I graduated from Cal Tech."

"Cal Tech." I whistled, impressed.

"Hey, look, I wasn't first in my class or anything—like Danny. Just a good girl who stayed up late doing her homework. You know Japanese-Americans—if you don't get straight

A's, your parents won't even let you go bowling on Saturday afternoons."

"Lucky I hated bowling."

"Me too." She grinned. "But there wasn't much else to do around Grant High."

"Encino, huh?"

"San Fernando Valley, born and bred. You know L.A.?"

"I lived there for fifteen years." I looked at her a moment. For the first time I noticed the redness in her eyes from crying. "You knew Danny well, I take it."

"Pretty well. I mean, as well as you could know him. He didn't like to talk about himself."

"Does this mean anything to you?"

I showed her the translation from the Polish message. She hesitated a moment. "Project Blowfish I don't know, but the 'Mania for Death' thing is a quote from Yukio Mishima."

"The novelist?"

She nodded. "Danny was very interested in Japanese culture. Kurosawa movies, Zen gardens. . . . He was always reading about it, particularly Mishima. He idolized him. The Bushido code. The suicide in front of the offices of the Japan Self-Defense Force. The whole samurai thing. He knew more about it than I did, that's for sure. He used to tease me about it."

"You think Danny could have committed suicide?"

"I don't know. He'd always go around quoting this work of Mishima's—*The Hagakure*. Actually, it was a commentary on some eighteenth-century writer . . . 'The Way of the Samurai Is Death.'"

"So that means he killed himself?"

She shrugged. "The closest I've been to Japan is the west coast of Catalina Island."

"And what about a motive? There'd have to be something more than a love of Oriental literature."

"Danny was gay . . . like Mishima."

"In this era of Gay Pride? When I was living in L.A., I felt like a dinosaur being heterosexual."

"I know, but he was very young. Everything happened to him so fast. An IQ of 170. A PhD at twenty-one. A millionaire at twenty-three. He didn't know who he was. He desperately wanted to be conventional in *some* way—at least sexually." She hesitated again. "I went to bed with him myself once but . . ."

"He couldn't."

She nodded. I traced her high cheekbones with my eyes. Anyone who couldn't get it up for this young woman was definitely *not* heterosexual.

"You're right," she said." It's a little crazy—someone committing suicide with a .357 Magnum. I guess I just liked him too much to think anybody would murder him." She stopped and stared at me again with those jet-black eyes of hers. I felt a tightening in my groin. "Look," she said, "if there's anything I can do to help you . . . if you need any technical advice . . . anything to find out what happened to Danny, I'll do it. Besides, Black Widow doesn't exist without him. He was the whole thing. He kept three quarters of it in his head."

It was then the door opened and Capshaw walked in.

He didn't know about Project Blowfish either, and as for Mishima, he thought the whole Bushido thing was a little pretentious. Danny was killed by the KGB for trying to help a Polish dissident. It was as simple as that. And after all, it was common knowledge that Poles would often come here on trade missions and then ask for asylum, usually to be turned down by the Americans for reasons of international diplomacy—unless they had a local sponsor. And someone as naive and idealistic as Danny would have been the perfect sponsor.

I left with the feeling that Capshaw's analysis was a mite too pat. It accounted in its way for the mysterious "Victor," but the rapid departure of Anna or Paula—the supposed dissident—

didn't make total sense. And my conventional detective instincts told me the demise of Nicky Li had to fit into this someplace. I tried to mull this over as I headed back to my office, but too much of my consciousness at the time was being dominated by the image of Laura Suzuki. This wasn't surprising. A few years before, I had fallen for a Chinese woman on a trip to the People's Republic, and I suspected I had an Oriental fixation as strong as Danny Rigrod's, although I doubted it was for the same reasons. In my case, twenty years of liberated American women had made me hunger for someone who would put out my slippers at night, even though, deep down, I knew it would bore me silly, maybe even embarrass me. But if they existed, those few Oriental women who combined that culturally supportive character with an unforced sense of equality and natural intelligence and wit were a stronger aphrodisiac to me than all the grass and ginseng I could consume at a thousand orgies. So I wondered about Laura Suzuki.

I kept wondering as I opened the door of my office to find a surprise visitor waiting for me there.

"Hello, M-Moses." The Wiz stood immediately, as if I were the chairman of the board of Tulip and he some cheap private dick they hired to plug a hole in the security department. "I h-hope I'm not disturbing you."

"I was the one who called—remember?"

"I know. I g-got here as soon as I could. I-I didn't even hear anything until this morning. I was in s-seclusion." He took a deep breath, a look of personal pain on his face as if some member of his immediate family had just died—or his oldest friend. "It's t-terrible, isn't it? He was a b-brilliant man. Extraordinary s-scientist."

"You knew Rigrod."

"Not w-well. I r-read his work in a technical magazine and hired him over the c-computer. I only m-met him twice. But somehow I feel responsible."

"Why?" I asked.

"This is my c-company. I started it."

"Any idea what this might be about?"

He shook his head.

"It's strange he would take a job for somebody else in the first place. I gather he was pretty well fixed."

Suddenly Wiz looked personally affronted. "B-Black Widow was a special program."

"Special how?"

"He could do whatever h-he wanted, s-spend as much as he wished."

"On what?"

"That was for h-him to decide."

"What about Project Blowfish?"

Wiz's face contorted awkwardly. "'Project B-B-Blowfish?'" He spit out the words with a triple stutter this time. "W-what's that?"

"Beats me. I found it written on a paper hidden in the apartment of this Polish girl he was hanging out with."

"Oh." For a moment he looked as if he'd been punched in the stomach. "Well, that's n-not important."

"Why not?"

"It's probably s-something Rigrod made up. He l-liked funny codes. It m-must've died with him."

"Suppose it didn't?"

"Then it d-didn't. It wouldn't m-matter anyway. No one but R-Rigrod could understand it."

"Not even Wiz?" I asked, eyeing him suspiciously and making no effort to disguise the sardonic tone in my voice. His behavior was certainly peculiar, but it was hard to know if it was the result of having something to hide or of a naturally paranoid personality.

"N-not even Wiz," the young genius replied, shaking his head. "R-Rigrod had a mind of his own," he added darkly.

Then he looked at his watch. "G-good-bye, Moses. I h-have to go back to my research. I c-can't let GTI destroy us. Then n-no one has a job."

"Sure," I said.

He started out.

"Wait a minute. Wait." I stopped him by the door. "Someone knew there would be trouble in Black Widow. I got this message on my computer. Signed Cassiopeia."

"What? The goddess?" Wiz sounded surprised. "There's a w-woman trying to tell you something?"

"Who knows?" I said.

He shook his head in puzzlement. Then he gripped my arm. I could feel his hand trembling through my sleeve. "You're doing a g-great job, M-Moses. Better even than I expected." And then he bolted through the door like a frightened deer.

Sharon—my area associate—walked in immediately afterward. "Wow," she said. "The Wiz came to *your* office!"

"Like God descending from the machine," I muttered under my breath, and headed out myself. I thought I'd go visit my friend Herb Shear and do a little horse trading.

The offices of DATTA Squad were on the third floor of the San Jose Police Headquarters. Originally two rooms, they had expanded to six and were moving like an octopus down one corridor and up another. I found Herb poring over a print-out report from the Customs Service when I walked into his office unannounced.

"How're ya doin', Trotsky?" Shear enjoyed addressing me that way since some guy in the department had showed him my FBI file. "Any more dead geniuses turn up in garbage cans?"

"Not so far. Look, uh, would you mind tracing down a phone number for me?"

He laughed. "Someone from Tulip wants *me*, a humble cop, to trace down a phone number?"

"This one's been erased from the sheet. Our computer turned up nil." I told him where I found it.

"A little breaking and entering, huh?"

"Hey, not me. I was just an honest citizen doing some apartment hunting."

"Look, Moses." He leaned in toward me. "We've got a problem here. I'm off this case just like you should be. This is homicide, for the murder boys. I know you were a private dick and everything but—"

"Do you want the phone number or not, Herb?"

"Yeah."

"Okay. Then this is what I want. You tell me the address of the disconnected number on that Polish girl's note and I'll let you in on everything I come up with. Otherwise . . ."

"Otherwise what?"

"Otherwise I never found it."

"Oh, shit. All right. Come on."

"555-7234," I said.

He got up and walked down the hall. Five minutes later he was back. "Let's go," he said.

"Where to?"

"Foster City. That address is up by Little Coyote Point."

We went up in separate cars because Herb had to be back in an hour and a half to teach his computer crime class at San Jose State. That was the one where he always threatened to use me as an example of how you could rise to the top of the security department of a major computer corporation without even knowing how to plug in the machine. I would tell him that kept me free of false preconceptions. And then we would laugh. Shear was a former Marine Corps engineer who went into police work out of conviction but, despite the fact that he thought I was a closet pinko and I thought he was a crypto-fascist, we usually got along. Maybe we were both further beyond ideology than we thought or maybe we were just getting older.

A fog was sliding off the Santa Cruz Mountains, creeping down onto the western shore of the bay, as I followed him off the Younger Freeway about thirty minutes later toward Little Coyote Point. Foster City was a rat's-nest town of about three thousand perched on the edge of the bay just above the Greco Islands. We continued past it down East Hillsdale to a dead end just below where the San Mateo Bridge crosses over toward Hayward.

No one was around as I got out of my car and legged it over toward Herb, who was staring out into the gloom of the point. "That's got to be the place." He indicated a small shack under the bridge a couple of hundred feet off. "The only address on East Hillsdale."

"Unless somebody blew it away when they changed the phone number."

Herb grunted his approval—something about that appealed to his aesthetics—and we walked down toward the shack, by now only half visible in the escalating fog. It was a tiny abandoned clapboard affair that looked as if it was about to fall down. "Typical GTI listening post, huh, Mr. Tulip?" That was another of Shear's games. He loved calling me by the company name because he knew my feelings about being identified with a corporation.

Not surprisingly, the front door had been padlocked shut. Herb took his pistol out of his holster and walked around to a side window. "Aha, typical police procedure," I said. "Always checking back for the warrant."

"You want in or you want in?"

"In," I said.

He smashed the window. A minute later we were walking around the three-room shack. It had been stripped as clean as Anna/Paula's apartment. I could hear the traffic rumbling by on the bridge overhead.

"Welp, dead endsky. I'll send the homicide boys over to take some prints."

"What about that?" I said, pointing toward a cardboard box that was peeking over one of the rafters.

I climbed up on a windowsill and handed it down toward Shear. He put it down on the floor and opened it up. The box was filled with brand-new Solidarity T-shirts.

"Somebody's cornered the market on Polish T-shirts," said Shear.

"Yeah, made in the Philippines," I said, pulling back one of the labels.

"Hey, everybody's for Solidarity—aren't you?" He looked at me. "No, I suppose *you're* for the *legitimate* Communist party of Poland."

"Absolutely. They represent the *true* will of the people, unbeclouded by the capitalist propaganda mills." I folded the box shut and handed it to him. "Here. Why don't you take this with you? It'll make a great visual aid for your class."

Shear grunted and headed for the door. "You coming?"

"Nah, I think I'll hang around and snoop about a little bit more. You mind?"

He hesitated. "All right. But if you get caught in here, you're on your own ticket."

"Hey," I said. "I wouldn't have it any other way."

Shear nodded and exited.

I went to the window and watched him drive off into the fog without noticing the late-model Mercury I had seen parked about a hundred feet behind when I climbed up for the box of shirts. As I expected, the door of the Mercury swung open and a heavyset man got out. I recognized him immediately although I had only seen him before for a split second. It was my friend "Victor"—the bastard who slammed me the other night in Alf Richardson's driveway.

He headed in the direction of the shack. I resisted the temptation to pick up a spare piece of board and give him back a solid dose of what he gave me and waited behind the window until I heard him slipping a key into the padlock. Then I quietly lifted myself over the sill and out of the shack, keeping low and moving as swiftly as possible toward my car.

I remained inside the car, keeping my head as low as possible on the seat for about ten minutes, until I saw Victor cruise by in the Mercury. I gave him as much leeway as I thought possible in the fog and pulled out after him. Ten minutes later we were heading north on 101 past Daly City into San Francisco. He continued onto 80 and then turned off again onto Eighth Street. I bypassed several cars and almost sideswiped a Toyota as I cut across two lanes to make the off-ramp before he disappeared in traffic. I followed him another three long blocks, when he drove into the Hertz office across from the Greyhound Terminal.

I pulled over to the side again. We were in the middle of the downtown business district—a serious tow-away zone—so I got out of the BMW and waited. When Victor emerged on foot five minutes later, I was ready. With a handy little pointer I quickly deflated my left front tire, flicked on the emergency light, placed a DISABLED VEHICLE sign on the windshield, and proceeded after him. It might not work but it was the best I could do under the circumstances.

Victor liked to walk. He took Market over to Hayes, Hayes over to Van Ness, Van Ness all the way up Nob Hill, stopping at a small jazz record store at the corner of Willow and emerging several minutes later with an album under his arm, and then all the way up to Vallejo. It wasn't done yet. He took Vallejo west another mile to Divisadero and then turned right. I was a block behind him, staying close to the wall, when he started to take an even more complicated course. He crossed Green, took a left on Union and then a left on Broderick, heading up toward Green alongside a seven-story Victorian red brick building that dominated that entire block of Pacific Heights. When he rounded the corner, I finally recognized it and froze, moving closer to the wall. I watched as he pressed a buzzer on the front gate, speaking into an intercom. It wasn't long before a guard emerged and admitted him into the inner sanctum of the Russian Consulate. Then I heard a whirring noise. I looked up to see a not-so-hidden television camera turning toward me. The lens zoomed on my face. I looked up and smiled, recorded for posterity. Or something. Then I turned and walked back down Divisadero. From a block away, I could see the huge radar dishes on the consulate roof trained on Silicon Valley.

The moment I was out of sight, I found a pay phone and called Shear, who had just arrived back from his class, and told him to pull his Soviet crib sheet and check out a Victor or Viktor. Then I mulled things over on the way back to my car. The Russian involvement in all this was as predictable as it was unclear. Did they kill Danny Rigrod? It made no sense. Even supposing that he had offered them some information and then reneged, it would seem pointless for them to risk an investigation for such small revenge. And who was Anna/Paula? Was she a lure, as the box of Solidarity T-shirts would seem to suggest, or the legitimate article? And why would Danny Rigrod, a homosexual, be interested in her, unless, as Laura Suzuki suggested, he had this bourgeois hankering after conventionality hidden in his renegade computer scientist's soul? The key, it seemed, was Blowfish, that mysterious subscript of Black Widow that nobody, including the Wiz, appeared willing or able to explain.

As luck would have it, I arrived back at my car just as it was about to be towed away. I offered a hundred-dollar bill to the Chicano mechanic, who pocketed it, reminding me, "You still gotta pay the ticket, *gabacho!*" and took off, leaving me to reinflate my tire with an emergency compresssor I kept in the trunk for such purposes. It wasn't James Bond, but it was something.

5

WHEN I GOT BACK to the office, Sharon was all in a dither. "Eddie Capshaw called you," she said. "He says it's urgent. He wants to meet you for drinks at the Lion and Compass at five o'clock. It's four thirty now." She pointed to her watch, a digital job from Japan that flipped out of its band and turned into a toy robot when you pressed a button. Robots were in the air. "Aren't you going?" she said. "Maybe it's important. Besides, it *is* the Lion and Compass."

I shrugged, but went off anyway. Going to the Lion and Compass was a big deal, but only if you'd never been out of the ten-square-mile radius of San Jose. It was the new "power" restaurant, started by Nolan Bushnell, the father of Atari, because he thought you couldn't get a good *saumon blanc en croûte* in Silicon Valley. Such are the privations of life. But because it filled a vacuum, within weeks after its opening it became the center for some of the biggest deals in techland.

Capshaw was waiting for me when I got there, drumming impatiently on the bar near where a Videotext display provided instant access to any of the world's major financial markets.

"Moses, good to see you!" He extended his hand again, crunching mine in that viselike grip of his. He would've made a good linebacker for the Raiders. "Look, I'm, uh, sorry to bring you over here on such short notice but . . . any news of Danny?"

"Nothing substantial."

He looked around briefly, then nodded down the bar where a silver tray of white crustaceans was stationed next to a bowl of Mexican *salsa*. "Have you tried the Santa Barbara shrimp? Melts in your mouth."

"Not hungry. What's up?"

"Like I said—sorry to bring you down here but, uh, what with Danny gone, there's not much left of Black Widow . . . and I'm, uh, being recruited by National Semiconductor and I might not be around for a while so I, uh . . . "

"Get to it, Eddie."

He leaned over toward me and spoke conspiratorially. "Did it ever occur to you that Danny could've been working for the Japanese?"

"Which Japanese?"

"I don't know . . . some company. He—" A couple of investment types in Armani suits sauntered down in our direction and Capshaw stopped abruptly, then continued in a loud, stagy voice. "Yes, that Santa Barbara shrimp *is* terrific! Beats anything I've tried—even in *Guaymas, Mexico!*"

I grinned. He was about as subtle as a stripper at the Royal Ballet.

"Not so good, huh?" He frowned as the men edged past us. "You'd think I'd be better at it for a military brat. Oh, well, National Semiconductor isn't recruiting me to be their security director, are they? Anyway, about Danny. He had these theories about the Japanese—that they were going to take over the world through the back door while the U.S. and the Russians bickered among themselves. You know, like aikido—that martial art where you take your opponent's power and use it against him. . . . It was almost as if he were rooting for it to happen. Like they deserved it or something."

"So you think he was giving them information."

"I don't know. It wasn't his style, but look, suppose he had been helping them and then pulled back? I mean, you're the expert, but couldn't they have gotten angry—or needed to make sure he'd keep quiet? Especially after all that bad publicity from the Hitachi business a couple of years back."

"As far as I know, anything's possible. You have something specific or is this just a theory?"

"Not really . . . although he did brag to me that he had important connections in Tokyo."

"What kind of connections?"

"He never mentioned names—just said they were better than we were, that they took the long view . . . understood history. But Danny never had a true grasp of the international situation. He was naive. He—" Capshaw broke off again as another man approached us. He was your basic technoid in a short but definitely non-punk haircut with about a half dozen ballpoints protruding from one of those awful vinyl holders in his shirt pocket. "Moses, this is Mr. Carruthers of National Semiconductor. Mat Carruthers, this is Mr. Wine of Tulip."

"Good to meet you, Mr. Wine." He shook my hand with an eager Rotarian pump, then turned to Capshaw confidentially. "Not another of your errant knights from the lamented Black Widow."

"Oh, no," said Capshaw quickly. "Mr. Wine's in our, uh, accounting department. . . . Great running into you, Mose." He slapped me familiarly on the back and winked. "We'll have to continue our little discussion later. . . . Sorry. . . . Think Japanese."

"Right."

I left feeling like I had just escaped a bad meeting of the Kiwanis—three hours long and very boring. And equally as useless.

On my way home I stopped off at another pay phone and called Shear again.

"Who's Victor?" I asked him.

"Don't know."

"They got to you already, huh?"

"What do you mean?"

"Never mind. Look, do me one last favor and tell me who he is and I'll never bother you again. Come on, Herb, you guys've got 3-D photographs, voice prints, and teenage diaries of every Slavic foot soldier who ever walked into that consulate, and the bastard *did* give me a two-day headache."

"His name is Viktor Maximov. Age forty-six, but doesn't look it. They call him Dr. Bebop because he loves American jazz and he's first-level GRU—Russian military intelligence— licensed to operate anywhere in the world. But if I ever hear where you found this out, I'll cut you one limb at a time with a Texas chain saw, starting with your cock!"

And then he clicked off before I even had a chance to say thanks.

When I arrived home, I saw a Rabbit convertible parked to the side of my driveway. Laura Suzuki was sitting on my front step, looking tired and distraught. She got up and walked over to me as I stopped my car.

"You all right?" I asked, getting out.

"This thing is starting to make me crazy." She shivered and clutched herself, although a strong late-afternoon sun had pushed its way through the fog. "I guess I'm having a delayed reaction."

"How about a stick of Château Neuf de Moses—guaranteed to soothe the soul and bend the mind?"

"Sure." She smiled. "Your generation likes that stuff, doesn't it?"

"Now don't get nasty." I reached back into my glove compartment and pulled out a joint of Poona Gold straight from the Big Island, lit it, and passed it over to her. It wasn't bad dope, just enough to give you a buzz without messing you up.

She took a hit herself. "You know, I've been thinking about

Danny. Maybe it's possible. Maybe he did keep some kind of record about Blowfish."

"But where?"

She shook her head. "I don't know. He had his own Zen garden. It's where he'd go when he wanted to . . . " She gestured with the joint.

"Center himself?"

"You could say that." She was starting to unwind and look around her. "I like your car. Does it have bullet-proof windows?"

I grinned. "Nope. It's all show—and it's not even mine."

"The Wiz, huh?"

I nodded. "Why don't we take a ride in it—to this Zen garden?"

We got in and I followed her instructions, heading farther up into the mountains. In a few minutes we were on a narrow winding road not unlike the one leading to Rigrod's old house. Laura directed me to pull over by an old hitching post and we continued on foot down a dirt path that skirted the side of the mountain. It went on this way for a while, through some heavy underbrush, and then came to a dense thicket. Laura took my hand as if it were the most natural thing to do and led me through a small passageway out on the other side by a stand of tall trees. We were facing westward now, toward Palo Alto and the ocean, and the sun setting through the fog bathed us in a pale golden light.

"Look." Laura pointed to a granite outcropping jutting out of the ground in front of us. It was oddly shaped yet somehow striking. A flat field of pebbles, raked in an even concentric pattern, circled around its base where a small bonsai tree had been planted. "That tree represents the forest at the base of Mount Horai. The crevice in the rock is the waterfall that plunges to the Central Sea, represented by the raked pebbles. Most Zen gardens do that—symbolize nature in miniature."

"I thought you didn't know much about your culture."

"Danny explained it to me." She walked over to the edge of the pebbles. "Most evenings around this time he'd come here and meditate—sometimes for a couple of hours. . . . I thought maybe if we reproduced his behavior, we'd find what we were looking for."

Laura looked at me. Like most Californians, I had tried meditation at one time or another, but it never gave me much more than a sore ass. But I figured—what the hell, I had done stranger things in my life, so I took a final hit on the second joint I had on our way over and walked over to her. She assumed the lotus position on one side of the rock and motioned for me to take the opposite corner. I followed, sitting and stretching each reluctant foot over the opposing knee.

I sat there for several minutes, receiving no enlightenment whatsoever. Then I tried to figure what Danny would have done, though I didn't know Danny and this was something of an absurd exercise in the first place. Perhaps Danny would have concentrated on the leaf being blown against the front of the so-called Mount Horai. I stared at it a moment, then a moment longer, and then . . . maybe it was the grass or maybe it was the extreme discomfort I felt in the lotus position, but I started to feel light-headed. The leaf loomed larger and larger. The mountain became a real mountain to me with a waterfall pounding full force, spraying jets of foam out on the water below. I could hear Laura laugh. I turned ever so slightly in her direction and was startled to see her sitting there in the sun with her blouse off. The top of her body was beautifully formed, her breasts an almost translucent white against the black of her freely blowing hair. She appeared to be in a deep trance. I started to smile.

It was then that I noticed the rifle. I didn't realize what it was at first. I thought it was just a strange metallic branch, pointing in my general direction from the trunk of a quaking aspen. But then the angle of the barrel lowered toward my chest and I hit the deck, shouting to Laura just as two bullets whistled within inches of my head and ricocheted off the granite surface of "Mount Horai," sending tiny pieces of rock shrapnel flying in every direction. I rolled across the pebbles, grabbing Laura and pulling her into the brush on the opposite side. Two more bullets scattered the stone behind us. Then pebbles crunched as a figure raced across the far end of the garden, leaped over a log, and disappeared into the trees on the other side.

We crouched low in the brush and waited. Laura covered her naked chest with her blouse. I looked for the man. I couldn't decide whether he wanted to kill us or scare us off. The latter appeared more likely. Two people meditating seemed the very definition of "sitting ducks." But there was no way I was going to test it out. We remained still for another five minutes, then slipped away as quietly as possible into the brush.

Twenty minutes later we were back in my house. Laura was pretty upset and had a few minor cuts and abrasions on her skin from running through the brush. The back of her blouse was ripped down to the bottom seam. I got her a faded anti-nuke T-shirt and she went into the bathroom to shower while I poured myself a tequila and stared out the window. By now it was pitch dark. For the first time it occurred to me that my lonely house in the mountains was relatively undefended. I looked over at Toto, wondering if he was of any use. Not likely. I was about to pour myself another tequila when I heard Laura singing in the shower. It was a strange and extremely rapid reversal of mood. She was singing opera, not brilliantly, but not badly either. It sounded like the end of *Madama Butterfly*, the part when the American officer returns to find his beloved geisha committing suicide. That was the part that always made my grandmother cry.

I took my second tequila, my mind ruminating over the water splashing down over Laura's twenty-four-year-old body, when I noticed the computer terminal blinking at me again just as it had a few nights before.

```
Welcome, Moses, Do you want to retrieve
your messages now? Y/N
```

I typed Y and a brief note quickly appeared on the screen:

```
Message  #2,  8:37:18,  Wield  the  long
sword in wide spaces and the short sword
in  narrow  spaces,  Do  not  look  for
blowfish in your local sushi bar, Beware
the  black  curtain  man  on  Warplanet
Street,
```

```
Cassiopeia
```

Cassiopeia again? Black curtain man? Warplanet Street? What the hell was all this about? I didn't even have a split second to think about it when a sudden bansheelike screech sent me spinning around.

Toto had gone on "alert mode," his pincerlike claw raised to full extension.

I went to a drawer where I kept a .38 in case of emergencies and backed up against the door beside Toto, whose lights were flashing on and off menacingly. I cocked the gun and waited.

After a few seconds a voice pierced the door. "Dad?"

"Jacob?"

I put the gun down and opened the door. My sixteen-year-old son was standing there, an overnight bag in his hand, next to a tall, athletic girl about his age who resembled Mariel Hemingway.

"This is Julie," he said.

"Hello, Julie," I said, ushering them into the house.

"You're the detective, huh?" she said, shaking my hand as if I were a specimen from her biology class.

"We, uh, decided to take you up on your invitation. It's President's Weekend and Julie wanted to try out her new Rabbit."

I wondered where Julie's Mormon parents thought she was as Jacob nodded through the side window to a brand-new car parked at the end of the driveway. "Hey, what's that?" he said, pointing toward the robot.

"Toto. Better watch out or he'll zap you with his ray gun. Toto, at ease."

The robot's lights stopped flashing and he lowered his pincer. The kids laughed, but then Jacob's mouth dropped open. Laura had emerged from the shower and was walking toward us, toweling off her long black hair.

"Julie and Jacob, this is Laura. . . . Laura's an engineer with Tulip."

"Hi," she said.

"Hi," they replied.

"Jacob's my son." I could see that he was impressed. Judging from the circumstance, he must have thought Laura was my latest girl friend. Usually my women left him cold, but Laura, I realized, was a good seven years closer in age to him than she was to me—and with her wet hair and pointed breasts jutting through the anti-nuke T-shirt, she looked nothing short of sensational.

She compounded the confusion when she took me by the arm and said, "Your father's an extraordinary man."

"Laura and I just ran into a little trouble," I explained. "Someone took a couple of pot shots at us while we were investigating a Zen garden."

I filled them in on the details over a dinner of fusilli smothered with a pesto sauce I found left over in the back of the freezer. We consumed a bottle of Fetzer Zinfandel at the same time, Jacob and Julie feeling very grown up having a couple of glasses each. From the looks of Julie, it might have been a first for her. But then, given the way she casually rested her hand on my son's knee, I couldn't be sure.

"God, Mr. Wine," she said, "I mean Moses . . . you think the Blowfish information is hidden in that garden someplace?"

"I don't think anything," I said, uncorking another Zinfandel. It wasn't so much that I wanted to corrupt youth as that I wanted to tie one on myself. Heavy adolescent libido was in the air and it was catching. And the more I sat there, the more attracted I was becoming to Laura Suzuki.

After dinner we got to hear something of Julie's rebellion against her Mormon parents. At that very moment they thought she was at a friend's house in Santa Barbara, Julie having conveniently left an incorrect phone number in case her mother decided to check up on her in the middle of the weekend. I listened to this, keeping one eye on Toto, whom I had put back on "alert mode," and one eye on Laura.

Soon Jacob and Julie excused themselves—it *had* been a long drive—and disappeared into the guest bedroom. I could tell I was being put in the role of hip, permissive dad, but at that moment I couldn't have cared less. I was wondering if Laura was going to get up and leave. She got up, all right, but not to leave.

"Let's go to bed," she said.

I followed her into the bedroom, only then for the first time thinking of Sara. She was up in San Francisco that evening, having dinner with some investment bankers, so I doubted she would pay me a surprise visit. But it wasn't unlikely she would call, so I took the phone off the hook.

"Expecting someone?" said Laura, noting my action.

"A friend."

"Don't worry," she said, starting to unbuckle my pants. "I won't tell."

"But maybe I will." I pulled the faded anti-nuke T-shirt from her shoulders and rolled with her onto the bed. I could feel the down comforter flatten beneath me as I slid out of my pants.

"What's your next move?" she asked, moving over on top of me and reaching down for my cock.

"Can't you guess?" I replied, stroking her thigh, the back of my hand brushing against hers as I began to caress the outer edge of her labia.

"About Blowfish."

"About Blowfish?" I laughed. "About Blowfish?!" She had to be kidding.

6

WITHERSPOON CERTAINLY WASN'T when he took me off the case altogether the next morning.

"I didn't know when I came to work for Tulip that it would turn out to be a government job," I told him.

"Don't get touchy, Moses. In the corporate world you have to learn to roll with the punches. Besides, my informants tell me there's nothing to be done about this Rigrod business. He was playing around . . . above his head . . . and whatever it was all about died with him."

"Died with him? I almost died with him! Who do you think took a pot shot at me yesterday?"

"Come now, Moses. You told me yourself they were only trying to scare you."

"Scare me from what?"

"Who knows? Look, whatever it was, forget it. Get back to your normal work and I can assure you no one's going to be using you for target practice." He fingered one of those little expensive desk toys they sell on the back pages of the Horchow catalog. "Unless, of course, you'd prefer to quit."

So that was what he was after.

"Maybe I will," I said. "Maybe I'll do just that."

And I walked straight out of his office.

Five minutes later I was standing in front of Delores, the Wiz's area associate, a motherly type in her late fifties who seemed more like the executive secretary for a small accounting firm than the aide de camp of a wunderkind. She was hunched over a computer terminal, looking frustrated.

"Moses, am I glad to see you!" she said.

"Where's Wiz?"

"I'm playing Deadline. You know—the computer mystery game you have to solve in twenty-four hours. Do you know the solution?"

"I need to see Wiz, Delores."

"It says Mr. Marshall Robner, the industrialist and philanthropist, was found dead in his home from an overdose of Ebullion, a drug he was taking for depression. But according to the lab report, his teacup contained tea only and no traces of—"

"Where's Wiz?"

"In seclusion, of course."

"Of course. . . . Now tell me where he is. It's an emergency."

She looked up at me. "Something wrong?" The truth was suddenly dawning on her.

"Of course there's something wrong. Now where is he?"

"I'm not supposed to say. You know if I did, they'd hound him unmercifully. The Bulb would never get finished. GTI would dominate personal computers forever and we'd all be out of jobs! I can get in touch with him for you, though."

"Great. Tell him if I don't hear from him in twenty minutes, I quit Tulip."

"Really? Nobody ever quits Tulip."

"Don't tempt fate."

Back in my own office, I had a message from Sara: "Where were you last night? Called to see if you wanted to review chapter twenty-seven of the *Kama Sutra*."

"Pretty sexy," said Sharon.

Fucking a twenty-four-year-old Japanese-American, I thought. Or being fucked by her. I couldn't figure out which. Somewhere around three in the morning, I awoke with Laura sleeping soundly beside me, with the sudden realization that it was *she* who had led me to the Zen garden. And considering that Capshaw had warned me that Rigrod might've been working for the Japanese. . . . For a P.I., I was somewhat slow on the uptake. At the age of forty, with a little *Cannabis sativa* dulling my nervous system, I was already in my dotage. Still, staring at her soft, unblemished skin draped across the white sheet, I could see it was easy to make mistakes.

I was mulling this over when the lady in question walked into my office with the bright, excited expression of someone who had just discovered gold or passed an entrance exam.

"I found it," she said. "Or rather Eddie and I found it."

"Capshaw? What?"

"Blowfish. We just went into the main data bank first thing this morning, hit the Black Widow password, and asked. It's no big secret after all. It was there all the time."

Laura leaned over my shoulder and typed a few symbols into my computer terminal. A series of equations popped up under the title Proj.: Black Widow/Sub.: Blowfish.

"What's it mean?" I asked.

"Not much. It's the start of a new microcode for a thirty-two-bit microprocessor."

"What could it do?"

"Hard to know. It looks as if Danny didn't get very far with it. You could use it for a lot of things."

"Like what?" I looked at her.

"Good morning," she said teasingly. "You were out pretty early. Your son taught us how to make matzoh and eggs."

I smiled, thinking of Jacob making matzoh brei for a Mormon and a Japanese. I imagined they ate it with mayonnaise and soy sauce. "Actually, I was getting canned," I said.

"Canned?"

"Well, not really. They just put the Rigrod thing on ice. But back to this processor. In idiot terms, just what could it do?"

"As I said, it's hard to tell. It looks like something pretty simple . . . an advanced voice activator or something. A lot of companies have been working on that."

"An advanced voice activator."

"You know—to understand human speech."

"My robot already does that."

"This'd do it better." She shrugged. "More words . . . inferences. Maybe that's why he called it Blowfish—because it's an expandable system." She looked at me. "I guess they have a point."

"About what?"

"In taking you off it. It doesn't seem like much."

"I see. Print it," I said.

She nodded, and what there was of the Blowfish program came spitting out of the dot-matrix printer on the table behind my desk. It came to about four pages of which I could understand only the title.

"Thanks," I said, ripping the pages off the roll. "See you when . . . tonight?"

"Sure." She half smiled. "Gotta go." She kissed me lightly on the lips and left.

I was watching her cross the lawn toward the R&D building when my phone rang. It was the Wiz.

I met him ten minutes later inside the entrance to the Bulb computer factory. All around us, workers were feverishly constructing the assembly line, installing robots that didn't look at all like Toto, but were giant mechanical devices to bolt, screw, and nail, replacing humans in form as well as in content. With blinking lights and color-coded wires, the whole place looked like an immense Léger painting brought to life.

Wiz pulled me over to the side where, incongruously, stood several GTI computer terminals connected to a GTI mainframe in the basement which governed the operations of the new factory, a constant reminder that Tulip—with all its glamour—was finally small change in the mighty world of business machines. And fighting for its life.

"D-don't leave us," said Wiz.

"Then stop hamstringing me. Or is that what it means to work for a corporation?"

"S-sometimes. Even for the p-president."

"Yeah, yeah. My heart bleeds for you. Only this time somebody died, in fact more than one somebody if we count Nicky Li. Beyond that, a Polish girl disappeared, I've been shot at, and my guess is a number of people are lying for diverse reasons. You, my precocious friend, perhaps even among them."

"M-M-Moses."

"And now—according to your new CEO—as far as Tulip is concerned, the Rigrod case is closed."

"It's not c-closed."

"Then who do I believe—you or Witherspoon?"

"M-me."

"But who has the authority?"

"That d-doesn't matter. We'll f-find a way."

"Oh, really. Whose company is this, anyway?"

"T-Tulip is a p-public corporation. M-Moses, please."

A huge forklift moved down in our direction. For a moment

I had the suspicion it was headed straight for us, but then it turned, veering off down the next aisle between some conveyor belts.

"Okay," I said. "Let's start with this." I took out the printout and showed it to him. "Laura Suzuki—a programmer in Black Widow—says this is Blowfish."

"Laura S-Suzuki?" he repeated, as if the name meant nothing to him. Then he looked down at the pages. A disturbed look came over him. He walked over to one of the GTI computers and sat down, rapidly punching a number of keys. Within seconds equations were running across his screen like rafts down a river. Then he stopped and looked at me.

"Wh-who is she?"

"Like I said—a programmer at Black Widow. Japanese-American, twenty-four, graduate of Cal Tech . . . very attractive," I added.

"F-find out more. Now!" The last, unstuttered word came out so sudden and direct that I was momentarily taken aback.

"What's this?" I said, indicating the pages.

"Sophisticated g-garbage. Replacement data for a s-stolen code." He tossed it in a waste basket and signaled to a man in a hard hat who was moving between two assembly lines. "S-see you tonight."

"Where?"

"San Jose State auditorium. Eight o'clock. The B-Brisbane-Bradley Debates."

The Brisbane-Bradley Debates? Only the Wiz would've been interested in that recycled roadshow of sixties nostalgia.

7

I WAS WRONG. The Brisbane-Bradley Debates were a big hit—at least at San Jose State. I slid late into the fifth row of a completely filled, one-thousand-seat auditorium to find myself flanked on the one side by the Wiz and his date, Miranda Clasp—an ungainly, willowy creature four inches taller than he who studied biogenetics at Stanford—and on the other by Jacob and Julie. The audience was composed almost entirely of well-scrubbed college students who sat in rapt attention, studying the two men who paraded in front of them like archaeological remnants of an era that seemed as far off as the Bronze Age.

Stuck in time, I thought, we're all stuck in time, no matter how hard we try to adjust, as Giles Brisbane, his now gray, now short hair so well coiffed, beamed at his audience and repeated his updated litany of the last twenty years: "Youth, youth, youth is making a revolution in this country. The older generation may want to stop it, but it's already happened—an electronic, asynchronous, totally democratic revolution forged out of computers and broadcast on MTV." I glanced over at his old nemesis, Scott Bradley, who appeared to be staring up the dress of the moderator, a talk-show hostess from a local television station. "And the Lenin, the Mao Zedong, of this revolution," continued Brisbane, "is sitting among us tonight." He pointed right into the fifth row. "Alex 'The Wiz' Wiznitsky—the man who made the power of high technology accessible to each of us in our own homes, breaking the stranglehold of big government and multinational corporations." A round of applause broke out for Wiz, whose face turned several shades of red. Brisbane grinned, clasping his hands over his head and walking down to the apron of the stage like an aging rock star: "Orwell was wrong: 1984 is not the year of Big Brother. It is the start of a new utopia—a youthtopia. I have seen the future, and it works!"

He gestured for more applause. If there was one thing you could say about Brisbane, he was shameless. I had first seen him speak about fifteen years before, when his hair was down to his shoulders and he was the international guru of psychedelic drugs, and even then he was milking his situation for all it was worth. Bradley was then the CIA's leading kamikaze pilot, willing to do or say anything for God, country, and the presdient. Now these two old warhorses needed each other more than Abbott and Costello.

What the hell—it all came down to making a living in the end. But if there was something sad about this, it was the audience itself—a generation truly without heroes or ideals of its own. Whatever could be said about their pot-smoking, protesting parents, at least *they* had a culture.

I watched as Bradley got up and began to do his song and dance, manufacturing whatever leftover anti-hippie bile he could still dredge out of his desperately trim, Nautilus-machined body, and leaned over to Wiz.

"She's gone," I said.

"Wh-where?"

"I have no idea. Her apartment's stripped like Anna Wajda's. She has no close friends. No one in the company knows where to find her, and she left no forwarding address."

"Oh, J-Jesus!"

"More amazingly, I don't have the faintest who she really is. She went to Cal Tech, all right, but Grant High has no record of a Laura Suzuki existing before the eleventh grade. And her parents don't seem to have existed. It's as if she materialized out of nowhere."

Wiz made a fist, grimly striking his forehead. "Oh, Moses, this is t-terrible."

"What'd she take?"

"I d-don't know."

"You don't know? Come on!" My voice exploded. Several people in the adjoining rows turned around. I had had enough of his stuttering bullshit. But Wiz simply looked down, staring at the tops of his New Balance running shoes.

I sat there fuming. By now a question-and-answer session was beginning, audience members lining up at aisle microphones to ask questions of the two great social philosophers. An angry redneck type around forty was taking the opportunity to harangue Brisbane, blaming him for the death of his sister who jumped out of the window during an acid trip in 1971. Another man instantly leaped to Brisbane's defense, claiming that during his two-hundred-plus acid trips he never wanted to do anything more violent than eat wild strawberries and listen to Creedence Clearwater. I waited for Wiz to say something. Finally, I just got fed up, told Jacob and Julie I'd meet them outside, and walked out into the lobby.

It was lined with production posters from the last ten years of the San Jose State Drama Club—everything from *Charley's Aunt* to *Arturo Ui*. I stared at them in the semi-depressed manner I had stared at the punk-rock posters on the wall of Laura Suzuki's barren apartment that afternoon when Wiz appeared, standing behind me.

It was another couple of minutes before he said anything. "M-M-Moses, I know something abut B-Blowfish."

"Surprise, surprise," I replied.

Again he hesitated, only speaking when I was about to turn him on again. "It was a special p-project . . . for the f-future . . . an extra chip for the B-Bulb."

"An add-on," I said.

Wiz nodded. "Very p-powerful . . . to m-make in a c-couple of years—when GTI c-came out with their new p-personal computer. We'd out-f-fox them, hop up the Bulb to 2000k of RAM. D-do things at home n-nobody every dreamed of."

"What things?"

"Everything. Ar-artificial intelligence . . . knowledge p-processing."

"A dream chip, huh? I didn't know Tulip had the facilities for that. This Rigrod must've been some guy. Was he close to it?"

"I-I don't think so. I d-don't know what he had. It was so b-blue sky. . . ." He gestured up toward a firmament that didn't exist.

"But the Russians were interested in it."

"Maybe. But they w-wouldn't understand it."

"Why didn't you tell me this before?"

Wiz looked away. "T-trade secrets," he said. "I d-didn't want *anybody* to know we were w-working on it."

"Including your security director?"

"R-Rigrod made me promise, otherwise he wouldn't w-work for me."

"But Rigrod's dead."

"And n-now I'm telling you."

"It took you a while," I said.

"I'm s-sorry, Moses. If you want to quit . . ."

"I'm thinking about it."

"D-don't. Please. Find Laura Suzuki. F-find her." He clutched my sleeve with an intensity that was almost maniacal. "For b-both of us. You'll b-be glad. I p-promise you!"

"But don't you have any clues—any information about her?"

He shook his head as the lobby doors opened and the audience began to spill out of the auditorium. I could see the college students staring at Wiz, whispering to each other and pointing to him as they headed out into the night. I wondered if one would come up and ask him to autograph his computer.

Jacob emerged with Julie and Miranda Clasp.

"God, Dad," he said. "You get bored so easily."

"Do I?"

"I thought they were pretty interesting . . . especially the part about youthtopia." He shot me one of his sly looks.

Wiz took Miranda Clasp's hand and we started off for the parking lot. From the side, he looked like a little owl walking a stork.

"Julie 'n I've gotta get back," said Jacob, indicating his girl friend's Rabbit parked near Wiz's car. "We're going to leave now."

"You're going to drive back to L.A. *now*? It's nine P.M." I had a sudden image of my son splattered across Highway 101.

"We'll stop in Santa Barbara at Julie's friend's." He lowered his voice. "That way her mom'll never know."

"Uh-huh, well look, why don't I ride with you?"

"Ride with me?"

"I have to be in L.A. in the morning." I turned to Wiz, who was getting into his car with the awkward Ms. Clasp—as odd a couple as ever sullied the leather upholstery of a Mercedes turbo-diesel. "I'm going to go chase Laura," I told him. "I don't know where it'll take me . . . just don't cut off my credit card."

"D-don't worry," said Wiz, a broad smile of relief blossoming on his homely face like a flower in a dry desert wash. He shut the car door. "C-call me. Please," he continued, leaning out the window as he turned on the ignition.

I stopped him before he drove off. "Wiz, one more thing— why was it called Blowfish?"

"Y-you'd have to have asked Rigrod. I-I don't know."

"You mean you want me to go looking for something without knowing what I'm looking for and without being able to recognize it if I find it."

Wiz shrugged apologetically. I nodded and stepped away from his car. I could see Brisbane and Bradley, chatting amiably, strolling to their waiting limousine, as he drove away.

Twenty minutes later I was packing a bag with one ear to the phone, telling Sara I'd be out of town for a while. "Maybe it'll be good for us," I said. "A few days' separation."

"Maybe," she replied.

"It's good to get perspective."

"They say."

It was all quite civilized, maybe a little too civilized. But I shrugged if off and slid my passport into my jacket pocket; then a copy of *The Hagakure*—Rigrod's samurai ethic—into my suit-case and zipped it shut.

I did most of the driving down south, the kids passed out in each other's arms in the back seat of Julie's car. I felt a sense of relief, as if I were getting away from a claustrophobic corporate world back to my real self, even if that self was locked in its own grim moods and motley past. I was a man who liked to work alone. In the final analysis, I had chosen that.

California flew by in the night, the roadside truck farms and fluorescent gas stations a comfort to me. I knew 101 by heart; flatlands, then rolling hills, then water. Soon we were heading down past Santa Maria toward Gaviota and the ocean. I drove into Santa Barbara at two thirty in the morning and dropped Julie at her friend's house on Loma Cedro. Jacob and I checked into the Miramar Hotel by the beach.

The next morning he and Julie left me off at a rental car agency by the Ventura Freeway. I continued on to Grant High by myself. Driving over to Encino, I had the feeling I always did about the San Fernando Valley. I was supposed to hate that flat, ugly, smog-ridden stretch of proto-suburbia, but somehow or other I felt a sympathy for its residents, as if they were innocent citizens unfairly maligned for having the misfortune to live in one of the most ridiculed urban landscapes in the world. It wasn't an evil place, after all. It was only the valley, not Nuremberg.

Grant High was hardly a landmark of modern architecture, a squat, concrete monument to no imagination plopped down in that endless no-man's land known locally as North of the Boulevard. I pulled up in front of it, adjusted a tie that was a mite too elegant for the circumstances, and marched into the administration office with my most neurasthenic civil servant's demeanor.

The woman behind the counter had the dull, heavy-lidded look of someone who had worked so long in the public school system you wanted to bury her in a filing cabinet. She approached me as if my presence were an intrusion on her space somewhere equivalent to a sewer rat entering the operating room at Cedars-Sinai Medical Center during open-heart surgery.

"Uh, hi," I said. "I hope those files of yours are pretty thorough."

"Haven't thrown out much since I've been here." She took a step backward as if to say "Now what?"

"Yuh, well, I represent SORDJA—the Society for the Restitution of Disenfranchised Japanese-Americans." I presented her with a card I had made up at a print shop on Reseda Boulevard about a half hour before. She examined it suspiciously.

"You don't look Oriental to me."

I shrugged. "Job market—you know what it's like. I've got a PhD in sociology, but if you're not in computers these days, you have to take what you can. . . . Anyway, it's a good cause so . . . you remember how the Japanese were relocated to concentration camps during World War Two—even though most of them were good Americans?"

"No, I don't," she said.

"Oh, well, that's what happened. The Germans and Italians could stay right where they were—walking the streets of New York—but they locked up the Japanese behind barbed wire in a place called Manzanar in the Owens Valley. Took away their businesses and everything."

"The Japanese *are* good in business." She nodded in a surly fashion, indicating that she was afraid they were going to take her job.

"Not these Japanese. Those are your Sonys and Toyotas over there in the Land of the Rising Sun. These were just your ordinary papa-sans and mama-sans who ran the candy store in Pacoima—know what I mean?"

"So what do you want—a donation?"

"Nothing of the kind. Just the smallest favor. There was a student at your school about eight years ago named Laura Suzuki. Her grandmother—who would now be in her eighties—is entitled to a four-thousand-dollar grant from our organization in repayment for the appropriation of her strawberry stand in 1941. Now this grandma-san, unfortunately, passed away three years ago and it is now incumbent on us to see if there are any surviving relatives and, if so, to find them so they may divide the money—comprenay?"

The woman sighed deeply from overkill and walked over to the file. "Laura Suzuki, you say?" I nodded and entertained myself reading the notices on the door of the college placement office. "There's a mark on her file. Somebody called about her yesterday."

"That was me."

"Oh, yeah. Well, she was only with us in the eleventh and twelfth grades, then went to . . . Cal Tech." She shook her head. "They sure do study hard."

"What was her home address?"

"Seems like there were two of them." She carted the folder over and put it on the table in front of her. "Here. See for yourself." She pushed the folder in my direction. "I don't know what these Japanese want out of us now," she clucked. "Four thousand dollars—they already own the world!"

I looked down at Laura Suzuki's file. Her grades were straight A's, her extracurricular activities none. According to the records, there had indeed been two addresses—one in Encino, from where she registered, and the second, to which she moved at the beginning of her senior year. It was in Gardena. I knew it well—a Japanese neighborhood almost a full hour away, famous for its legal poker parlors and inexpensive wholesale nurseries. It would've been one helluva commute for a high school girl. I copied down both addresses and left.

The Encino street was only about five blocks from the school, but Laura's old address was now part of a condominium complex built in the last two years of the type catering to swinging singles—lots of wetbars and a swimming pool with enough chlorine to turn you albino.

I cut back to the freeway and headed down to Gardena. It was late afternoon already and the lights were beginning to illuminate the poker parlors. Laura's second address was a small stucco house on a side street behind a low, brick industrial building. I parked and approached the house slowly. The name K. ICHIKAWA was printed in neat red letters on the mailbox. Someone inside was watching the Japanese-language cable station on television. I knocked on the door and waited. After a moment an old Japanese man opened it, keeping the chain on the latch. From the way he was squinting, I could see he was practically blind.

"Mr. Ichikawa?" I asked.

"Yes, yes." He spoke with the flat California accent of someone born in this country and wore a pair of black suspenders over a faded yellow shirt. I looked down from it to his baggy trousers out of the 1940s.

"My name is Dr. Loomis. May I come in?"

"What for?"

"I'm a professor from Cal Tech."

"What?"

"The California Institute of Technology in Pasadena."

"Oh." I could see him take a half step backward, placing his right palm on the door as if he were about to shove it shut. On the wall behind him were a couple of old framed photographs—one, about forty years old, was a wedding picture showing a youthful Ichikawa in a starchy tuxedo with a shy young woman in a floral-print dress. The other showed the same couple, about twenty years older, holding a five-year-old girl in the driveway of what I took to be a Toyota dealership near an Orange Julius stand. A sign over their heads said GRAND OPENING. A Shinto priest was sprinkling something in front of them while a gaunt man in a black suit looked on approvingly.

"I'm looking for a former student of mine—Laura Suzuki."

"I do not understand you," he said, now firmly pushing forward on the door.

I quickly wedged my foot in to stop it from shutting. "I said I'm looking for Laura Suzuki. We're interested in offering her a teaching assistantship."

"I do not understand you," he repeated. "Please come again."

"That girl." I pointed to the picture. "Isn't she Laura Suzuki?"

"I do not understand. Come again, come again." But his body language belied his obsessive politeness as he leaned against the door with his shoulder, crushing outward. I felt a sharp pinch on the side of my foot, then something kicking swiftly upward as I went flying out the door, barely staying erect as I tripped down the doorstep onto the sidewalk. The door was slammed shut in front of me. A split second later the dead bolt locked into place and a pair of shutters closed on the living room window. I took another few steps down the walkway, looked back at the house, and smiled. Not bad for a guy in his seventies, I thought. I hoped I could do half as well at his age.

I headed back down the Harbor Freeway to the Hall of Records to check out the title on the Gardena address. I didn't think it would tell me much, but it was an obligatory procedure in detective work, the kind of thing that made me hate it in the past, but now I found a kind of reassurance, an almost Zen-like satisfaction, in such a task. I was even pleased to see that the same grumpy Chicano woman was taking the five-dollar fee at the registration desk. The house, it turned out, did not belong to Ichikawa or to any Suzuki but to an operation called the S.D.C. Holding Company—whoever they were. They had bought it in 1964—the year, I surmised, Laura Suzuki would have been five years old.

I didn't know how to connect any of this, but I decided that someone who knew Los Angeles better than I did might be able to help, and there was no one who knew it better than my aunt Sonya. Besides, I hadn't seen her for the long months I had been at Tulip, so I hit the freeways again for the traffic-filled drive out to the Venice Senior Citizens Center.

Usually, whatever pandemonium I found at the center was created by the senior citizens themselves, squabbling with each other about events and issues as old as they were—Mensheviks and Bolsheviks, social democrats and anarchists, orthodox and conservative, all going at each other as if the czar had deserted the Summer Palace and the Russian proletariat taken to the streets two weeks ago Thursday. It was at once refreshing and weird—all this energy locked in a time warp several times more severe than Brisbane and Bradley's. And they weren't making any money out of it either.

But this time, when I wedged my car into the alley off Rose Avenue and walked around the falafel stand onto Ocean Front Walk, another more minor form of chaos had overtaken the neighborhood. A half-dozen photographers were standing in front of the center, which had been cordoned off, a pair of klieg lights illuminating the darkening sky. A sleek Cadillac stretch limo purred by the door, a number of Venice street people having congregated around it, staring in at its snazzy accoutrements—television, remote-control stereo, and gnarled walnut bar.

Wondering what rock star had taken up the cause of the elderly, I hurried inside before anybody could stop me, only to discover within that the center of attention was my own aunt Sonya. She was dressed up more fancily than I had ever seen her in a black-sequined frock, and she was flanked by two even more elaborately dressed women of about forty who were decked out in trendy evening gowns right out of the window of some chic Beverly Hills boutique. They shared with Sonya, however, an obvious discomfort with what they were wearing, as if all three found themselves plunked down by accident in some distorted version of *Queen for a Day.* About two dozen aged denizens of the center stood watching them with awe and fascination as another woman made some final adjustments to Sonya's frock.

"Oh, my God, Moses!" She turned beet red when she saw me, as if I had caught her in the middle of some unconscionable act. "What're you doing here?"

"What'm I doing here? The question is what're you doing here? You look like Cinderella dressed up for the Gray Panther Ball."

"Ah, I'm such a hypocrite." She clutched her head in pain and walked over to me, taking me by the arm and pulling me aside. "I don't know how I can go through with it."

"Go through with what?"

The two younger women looked over nervously.

"The Academy Awards," she whispered to me.

"The Academy Awards!" I started to laugh but then remembered something. "You mean that documentary about the old Jews of Venice—"

"Right, right." She nodded. "I know. Awards are terrible—a betrayal. I told these ladies. . . ." She gestured to the women, who were walking toward us looking more agitated. "It's just like Stalin with the Stakhonovites—dividing the masses by making heroes of individuals."

"Please, Sonya," said the younger of the two women. "We're depending on you to go with us."

"So I can assuage your guilty conscience. You said you made this film to show the problems of old people and now you're using it for your own aggrandizement."

"Maybe that's true," said the other woman. "But this is a film about old people. Somebody's got to represent them."

"She's right, Sonya," I said. "Relax and enjoy it."

"You keep out of it. What do you know anyway? You're working for a *corporation* . . . heaven help us. Oh, all right, let's get on with it. As they say in the *Talmud*—that reactionary compendium of religious folklore—'If you must eat forbidden pork, then let the fat drip from your lips'!" She reached for a cardigan and started out with the two women. "So what do you want," she said, turning back to me, "Mr. Gray Flannel Suit?"

"I came down to ask you a few questions . . . and because I miss you, you old warhorse. I need someone to keep me on the straight and narrow."

"If you need a geriatric Trotskyite to keep you on the straight and narrow, boy, are you in trouble!" But she gave me a hug and we walked out of the center together with the two women. She introduced me to them—a filmmaker and an anthropologist—but they seemed a little too catatonic from the impending ceremony to acknowledge the presence of anyone more anonymous than Johnny Carson. "So what's your problem?" Sonya continued as the chauffeur held the door for her.

"Missing person. Japanese. Maybe an industrial spy."

"Oh, yeah. Come on in." She motioned me into the limo with them. "My nephew's coming with us," she said to the two women in a tone that brooked no denial, then she turned to the driver. "The Oscars," she said. "And step on it!"

The limo inched out slowly as I told Sonya about the picture I had seen on Ichikawa's wall. "What I need to know," I said, "is the identity of an L.A. Toyota dealership that would've opened around 1964 right next to an Orange Julius stand."

"That's easy," she said. "Big Wally's Downtown Toyota on Second and Fuller. It was the first real Toyota dealer after they had that factory store on Hollywood Boulevard."

"Big Wally?" The name didn't mean anything to me. Car dealers usually made a splashy appearance in the classified advertising section of the L.A. *Times* or on late-night TV riding around on an elephant.

"Disappeared a year later. The landlord kicked them out."

"Who was that?"

Sonya thought back for a second. "Must've been a Japanese outfit—the Sumisa Development Company. They're the ones who got a building up there now."

S.D.C., I thought. "Sonya, you're a genius."

"For that you call me a genius? Ask me something difficult— like who made the argument against economism at the Third International?"

The women laughed tensely.

Fifteen minutes later we pulled off the Harbor Freeway at Sixth Street, heading for the Music Center. We turned down Figueroa to First and in two minutes were stalled in a long line of limos that were backed up to the valet parking. A temporary viewing area had been erected where a couple of vacuous-looking TV types were interviewing the arriving celebrities. The two women were craning their necks for a look at a sexy starlet, who was cavorting for the cameras.

"Ah, the Third International," I said.

"Don't get smart," said Sonya. Then she grinned at me, patting her hair, which looked as if it had been plastered down with a coat of polyurethane. "So whaddya think?" she said. "Is

America ready for an eighty-year-old Jewish pinko movie star?"

I said good-bye and left Sonya and the women about a dozen cars before we reached the parking valet. We were only about a half mile from Second and Fuller and I wanted to have a look at the Sumisa Development Company before making the long trek back to Venice for my rental car.

When I arrived at a quarter to six, the fourteen-story building was still quite active, its thousands of mercantile denizens benignly unaware that the Academy Awards themselves were about to begin only fifteen short minutes away. The directory in the lobby listed over a hundred businesses, with Sumisa, the landlord, allotted only a scant three rooms on the ninth floor.

They were about to close when I got there. A heavyset black lady in an unflattering purple sweater was locking up some files for the night. Some company brochures were on the counter and I picked one up and started to ask her some questions when I noticed two Japanese men talking agitatedly in the next room. From the back one of them looked remarkably like Ichikawa. I stepped off into an alcove just as he came walking rapidly out carrying a small suitcase. As soon as he was through the door, I pretended to the puzzled black woman that I had forgotten something terribly important and followed him.

He got into a waiting limousine at the entrance to the building and started off. I followed along after him on foot, just barely able to keep up with the limo, which was stalling intermittently in the rush-hour traffic and the spill-off from the Oscars. I finally found a cab near the L.A. *Times* building and jumped in.

"Did you ever follow a car?" I asked the driver.

"No. But I seen it on TV."

"Good. Then you know what to do. Follow that one," I said, pointing to the limousine.

It wasn't much of a challenge. Although loaded with amenities, the average Cadillac limousine is notoriously underpowered with somewhere near the acceleration of a prewar Volvo. We followed it for a while as it crept into the dense rush-hour traffic heading south on the Harbor Freeway. The driver was doing a good job, so rather than make conversation I pulled out the Sumisa brochure and started to go through it. From the looks of the propaganda, it was a real estate firm, pure and simple, located in Los Angeles and Tokyo and spreading eastward in the United States and north and west in its homeland, with no mention anywhere of a parent company or subsidiaries in the electronics trade.

"Hey, they're goin' to the airport!" said the driver.

I looked up to see that he was absolutely right. We had turned off the freeway and were headed west on Century Boulevard toward Inglewood, a giant 747 gliding down over our heads at a speed only slightly above the car's. In a few minutes we were at LAX, its new two-tiered facilities getting the finishing touches before the onslaught of the Summer Olympics.

We followed Ichikawa around to the international departures building and he got out and went directly inside. I quickly paid the driver and headed after him. He went straight to the JAL counter and spoke with a clerk in Japanese. I glanced up at the television monitor and saw they had one flight left that day, leaving for Tokyo in twelve minutes. He was cutting it close for an international flight. But the clerk was being very solicitous, almost giving him VIP status as he took his suitcase and put it on the conveyor. For a moment it flashed through my head that I was watching Blowfish disappear in front of my eyes.

As soon as Ichikawa started off for the departure gate, I walked swiftly up to the JAL counter.

"I'd like a ticket on the seven-ten flight to Japan," I told the clerk urgently.

"I am sorry, sir, but the flight is fully booked and the passengers boarded."

"But I'm a friend of Mr. Ichikawa's," I said. "We both have reservations together."

The clerk looked at me strangely and typed into his computer. "I am sorry, sir," he repeated. "There is no Mr. Ichikawa on this flight."

"But I just saw him here on my way in. He was buying his ticket a minute ago." I nodded in the direction of the departure gate.

"That was not Mr. Ichikawa."

"It wasn't? Who was it, then?"

The clerk looked at me again. This time his eyes began to glaze over. "We cannot give information on our passenger list, sir," he said finally, "without prior authorization."

I left him immediately and headed off toward the departure gate after "Ichikawa," rounding a corner and coming directly to the security check. A large sign warned that you couldn't go any farther without a ticket and I flashed something at the security guard, but it didn't wash. Two large uniformed men started to approach me and I backed off just as I saw "Ichikawa," about fifty yards ahead of me, boarding at the gate of his plane with a young woman. It was Laura Suzuki. They were the last two on, the gate closing behind them.

I ran back to the ticket area. There was one flight left to Tokyo that evening, on Pan Am, leaving in two hours. I bought a ticket, telegrammed the Wiz, hopped a cab back to Venice for my rental car and suitcase, and was back at the airport with thirty minutes to spare for the flight.

Nine o'clock at night on Monday the ninth of April I was on my way to Japan. It was only two in the afternoon over there.

8

MY FIRST IMAGE OF Japan was the smiling countenance of a hostess at Narita Airport who bowed and nodded to me several times, carefully pointing me in the direction of Customs as if I were a retarded six-year-old who had accidentally wandered off an international jetliner. I had spent my time on the plane sleeping and reading *The Hagakure*—Rigrod's favorite work— which mixed opaque Oriental philosophy with practical short-term advice like some eighteenth-century self-help book. "Silence Is Best," it told us. And "Start the Day by Dying: Absolute Loyalty to Death Must Be Worked at Every Day." My head continued to spin with these and other aphorisms as I dutifully followed the crowds down the glass corridors and along the people movers past endless Sanyo, Sony, and Hitachi signs to Customs and the baggage-claim area. I knew it was eight o'clock at night but my body wasn't sure which night. As the Customs officer examined my passport, I remembered the book saying "Do not form fixed opinions. It is wrong to have strong personal convictions."

The officer stamped my passport and waved me on quickly, alleviating a certain tension, because I had not had time to obtain a formal visa. Thus, on the plane I had taken some precautions filling in my landing card. Where it asked for purpose of trip, I wrote simply "tourism." Where it asked for occupation, I wrote "insurance," though after reading in

Rigrod's book, I had considered writing "*ronin*," or masterless samurai—that lone figure of solitary adversity. A man could profit from being a *ronin*, it said, but only if he did not remain one for too long. Fortunately for me, I was now a full-fledged samurai, serving my *daimyo*, Lord "Wiz" Wiznitsky of the Tulip Clan.

And he was a rich lord, I decided, so I drew several thousand yen with a company American Express Gold Card and took a hundred-dollar cab ride to one of the most expensive hotels in town. The driver didn't say a word for the entire trip, just clutched the wheel with pristine white gloves and stared straight ahead of him while I gazed out at the terraced hills of what the map told me was the Chiba District.

Ninety minutes later I was standing in a Japanese robe at the window of my room on the twenty-fifth floor of the Imperial Hotel, staring out at the endless pulsating neon of Tokyo. From my perspective, it looked like a gigantic pinball machine—a bigger, more powerful city than any I had ever seen—bigger than New York, London, even Shanghai, which I knew had a greater population. But this . . . If someone wanted to vanish here, especially from a foreigner whose knowledge of the language was limited to please, thank you, and *nigiri sushi*, it would be laughably simple. I thought about this a moment, then took two hits on the diminishing stash of Poona Poa I had stuffed in my shoulderbag and collapsed on the bed like a dead man.

I was awakened late the next morning by a chambermaid who, having mistakenly entered to make up my room, immediately covered her mouth to suppress a giggle and retreated amidst a flurry of bows and " 'scuse me's." I called room service for breakfast and then groggily rolled out of bed for that morning's *Japan Times Weekly*, which had been slipped under my door. Although I knew it would be highly risky, I had no choice but to find a translator. I found what I was looking for in the want-ads of the paper: "BUSINESSMEN! Your voice in Tokyo. Call JAPOTRANS—444-6802." I dialed the number.

I was met by a Mr. Yamamoto—an extremely courteous man—in a fifteenth-floor office opposite the Fuji Bank Building. Everything was clean, simple, functional, decorated with a few international travel posters meant, I supposed, to flatter the clients.

"What kind of business are you in, Mr. Wine? Thank you very much," he asked me in clear, precise English, bowing slightly from the waist.

"Insurance. I'm here to settle a claim." I handed him a card I kept for such situations.

"I see," he said, examining it and bowing again. "Thank you very much. Is this a big claim?"

"No, no, very little. My company just wants to get it settled, that's all."

"Ah," said the man. "A small claim then." He bowed a third time, but in what seemed a highly perfunctory manner. "Then you will not want the translator very long."

"No. That's not true. Insurance claims can be tricky. Even small ones. I need someone who can be available at all times. Night, day, whenever."

"Thank you very much," said Yamamoto, now bowing enthusiastically. "I will think of this for you. I will think of this for you." He stopped a moment to think of this for me. "I think there is someone here right now who would be very good for you, thank you very much . . . Mr. Hodaka."

"Mr. Hodaka?"

"Yes, Mr. Hodaka excellent translator. Translates books. Is writer himself."

A writer, I thought. Not a terrific idea.

But Yamamoto was already pressing a button on his desk. "I will get him for you right away."

A man appeared within seconds, as if he had been poised,

waiting behind the door. He was a handsome, slightly dissipated type in his late forties with long, silvery hair and dark, sensual eyes. He wore faded jeans and a trendy jacket of cracked leather with a number of zippers running in different directions.

"Mr. Wine . . . Mr. Hodaka. Mr. Hodaka . . . Mr. Wine."

Hodaka didn't bow, but thrust out his hand to shake with a simple "Hello."

"Mr. Wine is in the insurance business. He wants to settle a claim." Hodaka nodded perfunctorily, clearly unimpressed. "He needs you to be available day *and* night," Yamamoto added pointedly.

"Day *and* night, Mr. Wine?" Hodaka's sudden smile revealed a pair of gold teeth. "You want to see Tokyo day *and* night . . . that is my specialty."

I think he had the wrong idea straight off, but I figured we could straighten that out later. I said good-bye to Yamamoto, leaving him a down payment, and rode down the elevator with Hodaka.

"What company are you with, Mr. Wine?"

"All-Weather Insurance."

"Lucky fellow to come to Tokyo by yourself. Are you married? This is a man's world. Hodaka will show you."

"Later," I said. "Right now we have to go to the Sumisa Development Company." I showed him the address.

"Insurance," he muttered.

We got into a cab and Hodaka gave instructions to another driver in pristine white gloves. Identical white doilies were tucked neatly over the front seat, and the chrome on the ashtray covers was polished to a gleaming shine. For its size, this city was the cleanest place I had ever been. It was as if they sterilized it every morning for some mass operation. But it was also incredibly crowded. Within seconds we were stuck in the biggest traffic jam I had ever seen. The whole city had turned into one big parking lot, Toyotas, Hondas, and Isuzus stacked up as far as the eye could see. "How long is this gonna take us?" I asked.

"An hour . . . hour and a half." Hodaka shrugged. It was money in the bank as far as he was concerned.

"How about the subway?"

"Six minutes."

"Let's go." I paid the driver and we headed with the human wave down into the subway. I followed Hodaka along a labyrinth of corridors, an underground city in itself with coffee shops, drugstores, ceramics shops, even fancy restaurants and boutiques on several floors right next to the train lines—but no graffiti or bums. In fact, nobody even looked poor.

Ten minutes later we were in the lobby of the Sumisa Development Company building in the Marunouchi District. Hodaka stared at me in amusement as I stood in front of the directory, which was written only in Japanese ideographs.

"Which department do you want?" he asked.

"I don't know. Is this all Sumisa?"

"Some Sumisa, some other companies. There is even a detective agency." He grinned. "I write detective stories . . . among other things."

"That's interesting," I said.

"They are not available in English. Someday, perhaps. . . ."

"Let's go to the main office of Sumisa."

We went up to the twelfth floor, the main offices of the Sumisa Development Company, which were considerably larger, although less opulently furnished, than their Los Angeles counterpart. Hodaka introduced me to a secretary as a representative of All-Weather Insurance from Burbank, California, and she went off looking for someone sufficiently responsible to deal with my visit while Hodaka and I waited in a cramped little area with three chairs and a coffee table.

"So what does Sumisa do?" I asked him.

"You don't know? Real estate development. Very boring business . . . like insurance."

"It doesn't do anything else? It's not one of those octopus creations of Japan, Inc., with a tentacle in every corner of the economy?"

"I do not think so," said Hodaka. "I have never heard of them. What is your problem with Sumisa?"

"Oh, nothing much. Just an automobile accident."

"And they send you all the way to Japan?"

"I come from a thorough company."

Hodaka nodded, but I could see he was perplexed as a tiny woman in a smock came and brought us tea. It was whipped into a green froth and tasted medicinal. A functionary of Sumisa arrived almost immediately thereafter. He was a homely man with crooked teeth and extremely thick glasses. He introduced himself as Mr. Kawashima and asked what he could do for me.

"Your company owns property on 23 Atkinson Street in Gardena, California, which is presently occupied by a Mr. K. Ichikawa, an employee of your company," I told him through Hodaka.

The man nodded noncommittally.

"An accident occurred there between an automobile registered in the name of Mr. Ichikawa and a moving van represented by my company. Considerable damages were caused to the van and to its contents."

Mr. Kawashima shook his head and asked why we did not deal directly with Mr. Ichikawa.

"Because he left for Japan yesterday, taking all his belongings with him."

Mr. Kawashima shook his head again, took a deep breath, sucked in some air through his teeth, and said some constricted words to Hodaka. The translator turned to me. "Mr. Kawashima wants to know what he can do."

"Ask him if he can find Mr. Ichikawa."

Hodaka complied, got his answer, and turned to me again. "He will try. He wants to know where he can contact you."

"Tell him I'm leaving the country tonight but to contact you."

Hodaka looked at me, now totally perplexed. "You are leaving the country tonight?"

"No, I'm not, but just do what I'm telling you. Give him your phone number. Tell him you work for my company or something."

"I work for *your* company."

"Use your imagination. You're a writer."

Hodaka looked at me again, nervously pushing back his long silvery hair. Then he smiled, turned to Kawashima, and started conversing with him for several minutes in Japanese. Kawashima said hardly a word himself but responded in deep, guttural tones, his face contorting as if Hodaka were reporting a death in his family or the advent of nuclear war. Finally Kawashima stood, bowed to me very deeply, and exited.

Hodaka turned to me on the way out. "I told him you were chairman of the board of All-Weather Insurance International, come here to train me as director of the Tokyo branch . . . and that if he didn't find Ichikawa, I would lose my job for sure."

"Not bad," I said. "I don't know if I could've done better myself."

"Okay," he said, as we reached the elevator. "So what's the game? Who are you, Jack?"

I grinned. "Let's say I do what you write about."

"Hah! I guessed it—an American private dick!" The elevator opened before us and we entered. "So where you wanna go tonight, Marlowe? A *sutorippu* show . . . a *nozoki* peep show . . . a *nopan-kissa*—coffee shop with bottomless girls? There are things in Tokyo you never dreamed of on Times Square or the Sunset Strip!"

For the moment we settled on a *soba* joint in the sub-basement of the local subway station. A half-dozen construction workers were noisily slurping cold wheat noodles from bamboo trays while keeping one eye on the television set, which was showing an interview with a sumo wrestler. An on-screen digital readout, courtesy of Seiko, kept track of the time so, I presumed, everyone would know when their lunch hour was over, no one wanting to be a minute late in this most punctual of countries.

When we sat down, I asked Hodaka to order us the noodles and a couple of bottles of Sapporo. I was feeling some jet lag and I wanted to take the opportunity to scope him out more carefully. I knew I would need allies in Japan and I knew, to some extent, I had to take what I could get. But I didn't want my eagerness to translate into a drastic mistake.

Our beers arrived and I eased into things by asking Hodaka some questions about his writing. He didn't want to admit it directly, but I could tell he was on to hard times. The detective stories he wrote were a thing of the past. Even his translating work was intermittent. Most of his income, he said with a resigned smile, came from pornography.

"Oh, yeah?" I replied, trying not to seem too surprised. "What kind of pornography?"

"Stories about Americans."

"Stories about Americans?" For a moment I thought he was putting me on, but then I realized: the "Mysterious West"— land of baseball, barbecue, and big boobs. It made complete sense. Besides, given my own vaguely racist proclivities, who was I to talk?

"So," said Hodaka. "Here we are—an American detective and a Japanese pornographer. Perhaps you will have an adventure and I will write your story."

"Perhaps."

He swilled some beer, looking at me. "Who sent you here? Not this All-Weather Insurance?"

"No. Not them."

"Then who?"

"American computer company."

He frowned. I slurped a few more noodles, dipping them first in a sweetened soy sauce and then sucking them in with a loud, snapping noise similar to my neighbor's.

"What is this? A case of industrial sabotage? You want to steal the trade secrets of a Japanese company for American advantage?"

"Or the other way around—a Japanese company already stole the secrets of an American company."

"Hjunnh." Hodaka himself now made a pained, guttural sound like his countryman, the Sumisa functionary.

"Problem is, the American government doesn't seem too interested in the company getting it back, for whatever reasons. And the Russians have their eye on it too—or they had."

For a moment Hodaka looked at me incredulously. Then he started to laugh. "You puttin' me on, Jack! You runnin' a scam."

"No scam," I said, amused at his use of the language which he seemed to have picked up watching Cagney movies on the late show.

"Hjunnh," he muttered again. "This is strange business."

"It is. You wanna help?"

Hodaka again nervously patted his hair. Suddenly he was looking quite old. He was one of those people who hovered precariously on the edge of stylishness, affecting clothes and fashions ten or more years younger than they were, in the hopes that they would preserve a fast-fading youth. There was a feeling of desperation about it, but it gave me a curious sympathy for the man.

"If it's bothering you," I continued, "I'd like to tell you I'm not anti-Japanese any more than I'm anti-American or anti-anything else. I wouldn't do this for the glory of any country. Nationalism to me ranks about two notches above child molestation."

"Then why do you do it?"

"It's a job. Besides, some people back in the States got knocked off for reasons I imagine were dubious at best. I don't like that."

"Ah, the code of the detective." He nodded to himself with a satisfaction that was almost literary. Then he said, "All right. I will help you, if I can. But I must tell you, I am not a very courageous man. Violence frightens me. I only write about things like that."

"I'm not asking for a bodyguard."

"Then what do you want?"

"I don't know yet." I hesitated for a moment, then thought of "Cassiopeia" and took a stab in the dark. "But for starters, do the words 'black curtain man' mean anything to you?"

"*Kuromaku?*" He laughed. "Where did you hear about them?"

"On my computer."

"Your computer tells you about Japanese politics?"

"Not usually. Someone left a message—'Beware the black curtain man on Warplanet Street.'"

"Warplanet Street . . . Warplanet Street." The reference confused him. I had decided to leave out any mention of Blowfish for the moment.

"So who are these *kuromaku?*" I said.

"This is hard to explain. Our systems are so different." He took a deep breath and glanced around briefly before continuing. "Basically, it is this: Unlike your country, corporations are allowed to donate unlimited amounts to individual politicians and parties—even to adopt them. But nobody likes to admit this. Nobody likes to admit anything here. This is a country where we say 'Never take yes for an answer.'"

I could understand what he meant. It reminded me of all the contradictory advice in *The Hagakure*. "So what do they do?" I asked.

He took out a pack of Peace cigarettes and offered me one.

"They make their donations quietly, through the faction leaders—what you call bosses—of the various factions of our leading party—the LDP." He lit his cigarette and lowered his voice. "Sometimes this money isn't all on the—how you say it?—up and up. You know: bribes, payoffs, undeclared contributions. We call that black money. And it gets passed to the politicians by fixers with underworld connections—the *kuromaku* . . . black curtain men."

"And one of them lives on Warplanet Street?"

"I doubt there is such a place."

"But there is such a planet—Mars."

"Mars . . . a warrior . . . an American candy bar. . . . " Then he brightened. "Kasei-dori—Mars Street in Akihabara. That has to be it!"

"Why?"

"Because it is in Akihabara—the electronics center of Tokyo. Surely you have heard of it. It is where every American goes to buy a cheap stereo."

Minutes later we were back on the subway, riding north on the Hibiya line for Akihabara. It was only three o'clock, still a couple of hours from rush hour, but the cars were already jammed with passengers and we had to be stuffed through the doors by professional pushers in white uniforms. But even in this sardinelike atmosphere no one shoved or kicked. Everyone was courteous and well-behaved. There was something eerie about it.

Going up the steps from Akihabara Station, we were in another human wave of Japanese. If every American came here to buy a cheap stereo, it was news to me. I seemed to be the only white face for blocks. Indeed, I had never been any place that seemed so homogeneous—not even China. The Japanese felt to me like one giant organism, living and breathing together. They didn't need a Marxist revolution. They had already cooperated voluntarily.

The immediate area near Akihabara Station was a normal

industrial mix of warehouses and small shops, but I followed Hodaka around the corner and within one block we were in a thicket of electronics outlets as dense as a Middle Eastern bazaar. Neon signs for Dynamic Audio, LAOX Computer, Radio Kaikan strained against the afternoon sun as they decorated the facades of a dozen seven- or eight-story buildings, some of which appeared to contain hundreds of businesses. Narrow streets ran off in other directions with open stalls selling all manner of modern consumer goods from laser disk players to portable vacuum cleaners. Other shops sold small electronic devices—resistors, capacitators, plus every conceivable computer product from disk drives to mother boards to microchips of both Japanese and American extraction. Some of those I recognized were only eighteen months old, not the latest thing but hardly geriatric, even in the fast-moving world of semiconductor technology. It wasn't a bad place to come if you wanted to put together your own missile guidance system or ultrasensitive, omni-directional spy satellite.

Hodaka turned a corner by the Hirose Audio Center and someplace called Nakaura Denki and we were on Mars Street. The buildings here all seemed computer-oriented with specialized parts I didn't recognize being sold in smaller stalls interconnected by mazelike corridors. Hodaka and I wandered among them, up and down escalators that connected the various floors, when the sight of a particular stall on the third floor made me stop short. CHRYSANTHEMUM COMPUTERS— TAIPEI & TOKYO, it said in both English and Japanese. Nicky Li's company, I thought, right here.

Hodaka watched as I stopped a few feet away and watched. The man behind the stall was demonstrating a Chrysanthemum One computer for a customer, booting up a spreadsheet program I recognized immediately as Tulipcalc—a standard piece of software with the Tulip Ii. It ran very well with the Chrysanthemum.

"Great computer," I said, wandering up to them.

"Yes, yes . . . good . . . good," said the man behind the counter. He obviously spoke some English.

"And a lot cheaper than the original." I glanced down at the price, which was 75,000 yen—slightly over three hundred dollars.

"Yes, yes . . . cheap, cheap. You want?"

"I'd have trouble taking it home with me. It'd be a violation of U.S. copyright laws."

"No problem, no problem." The man waved his hand in dismissal. "Every day go." I was sure he was right. Hodaka had come over, joining me at the counter. "So how many you want? Bring home friend." He leaned in toward me. "Sell to friend. Pay for trip."

"I dunno," I said. "I was planning on waiting to buy one of those new Bulb computers. I hear they're due next month."

"We have them already."

"You what? That's impossible. You can't even get them in the States."

The man grinned. "We copy prototype."

"Let me see one right now!" I sounded like an eager buyer and, indeed, I was eager to see this. Where could they have gotten it? As far as I knew there were only about a dozen Bulb prototypes in existence and half of them were in the hands of software manufacturers who were sworn to secrecy. The others were in locked offices—accessible only by card—back at Tulip headquarters in Sunnyvale.

"Not here," said the man behind the counter. "Not here." By this time his other customer had drifted off. Hodaka was watching me intently.

"Where can I see it?" I said.

"Tomorrow," he said.

"Tomorrow where?"

"Tomorrow I will tell you. Make order. We send." He was starting to make less sense. Did he really have a copy of the

Bulb for sale or was this the usual line of computer bullshit in which the company or the supplier tells you the product is immediately on the way so you won't buy from the competition—a high-tech version of bait-and-switch?

I turned to Hodaka. "Tell him I want to see their Bulb computer before I order one."

"Yes, yes . . . you see. Tomorrow," the man said, before Hodaka even began to translate.

"Tomorrow where?" I repeated.

"You phone," he said, handing me his card. It had the name of the company—Chrysanthemum—with a phone number in English on one side and in Japanese on the other. "You have card?" he continued as I shoved his in my pocket.

"No. No, I don't. I'm sorry. I'm just here as a tourist." Some tourist, I thought. Not long ago I had initiated an action that had resulted in the head of his company having his brains blown out. And for what—importing a few lousy computers? I felt an uncomfortable twinge of guilt about this and turned away when, out of the corner of my eye, I caught the figure of another Caucasian standing in the shadow of a diskette stall.

He bolted toward the escalator just as I made a move. Not wanting to disconcert the counterman, I nodded a polite good-bye while backing up discreetly and then headed off as swiftly as possible without raising suspicion. Hodaka followed, breathing heavily. He smoked a lot and I could tell immediately he wouldn't be the greatest ally in a chase. Under the circumstances, however, I knew it wouldn't make any difference. By the time I reached the top of the escalator, the Caucasian had already disappeared in the web of stalls below. And, in any case, I had known who it was the moment I saw him. Having received his fist in my face and on another occasion having followed him thirty miles in a car and then five miles on foot along the streets of San Francisco, for the rest of my life I would have no trouble recognizing the silhouette of Viktor Maximov.

"You know that man?" said Hodaka as we emerged in a duty-free camera shop at the bottom of the escalator.

I nodded. "Russian."

"Russian?" said the Japanese, his face a bewildered mixture of tension and eagerness, as if his fantasy life were about to break into reality. "Let's follow him!"

"Don't be ridiculous. The man's a professional—first-rank GRU. He's undoubtedly hiding somewhere, waiting for us to do that very thing. Besides, he knows who I am and is probably extremely surprised to see me in Tokyo. He could disrupt my work, kill me if he wanted to. The last thing I want is for him to know where to find me."

Hodaka frowned. "You staying at Imperial Hotel?"

"Yup."

"That is dangerous—easy to find you. Any hotel easy to find—especially for Russian spy." He coughed nervously a few times, thumping his chest near where his pack of Peace cigarettes bulged from his shirt pocket. "Perhaps you stay with me."

9

HODAKA, IT TURNED OUT, lived in two places—a small house in the country where he kept his wife and ten-year-old child, and a two-room office-flat in the Shinjuku District where he kept his mistress, Fumiko, and sometimes, I gathered, her friends Kazue and Sachiko, who worked in the area Hodaka vaguely referred to as the "fortune-telling studio downstairs." Where I would fit in this confusion I had no idea, but I was surprised and moved by Hodaka's hospitality and grateful for the opportunity to vanish quickly into the Tokyo netherworld— what they called the *mizoshobai*.

I learned about the fortune-telling studio later that evening. By the time I had checked out of the Imperial with no forwarding address and followed Hodaka on yet one more subway foray across the city, it was nearly pitch dark. Shinjuku, however, was ablaze with enough neon to read the fine print on a medieval manuscript. Two million people a day swarmed through the turnstiles of Shinjuku Station, and the main shopping streets were like the midway for some endless amusement park, barkers hitting on you from every side while a thousand Japanese-made "ghetto blasters" belted rock in a cacophonous blend of English and their native tongue. The whole place made Times Square look like the amusement area of a minor suburban shopping center.

Hodaka led me off the main drag down a series of side streets behind the Isetan Department Store lined with strip bars, massage parlors, and cheap eating places until we came to a little hole-in-the-wall with a gypsy fortune teller crudely painted on the door above some Japanese writing. Only there was something peculiar about it because the fortune teller was holding what appeared to be a hot dog in her hand instead of the traditional tea leaves and crystal ball.

"Is penis," said Hodaka, smiling as he opened the door. "She reads penis to tell future."

I followed Hodaka's gaze through a beaded curtain where a topless "fortune teller" was indeed reading the penis of a businessman who, absurdly enough, still wore his dark blue sports jacket and tie with his matching blue suit pants balled up around his calves. Hodaka was right—there were things in

Tokyo you couldn't find in New York and Los Angeles.

We headed up a stairway to the right, emerging in Hodaka's tiny apartment. It was furnished in a mixture of Western and Japanese styles, a shoji screen separating the kitchen–dining room from the living and sleeping area. A couple of young women in their early twenties I took to be Kazue and Sachiko were lounging on the sofa when we came in, and Hodaka scattered them with a wave as if they were so many irritating house pets. They went off into the dining room, staring back at me with meek curiosity. Hodaka sighed impatiently and pulled the screen shut behind them. I wondered how he would get along with the women I knew—fifteen years into the women's liberation movement. Not terrifically, I imagined.

But I was too tired to give any thought to anything, whether it be the conundrums of feminism or the death of Danny Rigrod and all it had engendered, and sunk in jet-lagged fatigue onto the vacated sofa. Hodaka excused himself and wandered across the room to his desk, which was pushed into a corner against a wall jam-packed with books. Within seconds he was typing away at a rapid clip on a small portable typewriter, telling tales, perhaps, of the famous erotic fortune tellers of Dallas, Texas.

My eyes began to glaze over and I am not sure how long it was before they focused again on the light blinking on and off outside the window of the apartment. At first it appeared to be an orange globe or, more accurately, a football-shaped object like a miniature illuminated blimp hanging over the doorway immediately across the street. Eventually, however, I recognized that I was staring directly at a brilliant enlarged model of a glowing blowfish. I sat up sharply on the sofa, a sudden jolt of adrenaline instantly erasing my jet lag. *Do not look for blowfish in your local sushi bar,* I thought. *Beware the black curtain man on Warplanet Street.*

I stood and walked over to the window. The blowfish was

indeed hanging over the door of a sushi bar, the skillful chefs visible through the window slicing raw fish for a crowd of customers, some of whom were standing in the back waiting to be seated.

"What's blowfish like?" I said to Hodaka, who was still banging away at his Olivetti.

"Blowfish?" he said.

"You know—the fish that's hanging over the sushi bar across the street."

"Ah, the *fugu*. . . . You call it the globe fish, no?"

"Or the blowfish."

"Very expensive." He pulled a sheet out of his typewriter, looked at it in disgust, and tossed it in the wastebasket. "And dangerous. You can only buy it at special sushi bars where the chef is licensed by the government."

"Licensed for what?"

"To prepare the *fugu*. It is a great delicacy, but parts of it are poisonous. Only those skilled in its preparation know how to separate them properly. Even then there is some risk. A few years ago a famous Kabuki actor died in a bar like the one across the street."

I looked down at the bar again. The patrons didn't seem concerned. Blowfish, I wondered. Why had Rigrod named it Blowfish? Simply because it was poisonous?

I wandered back to the couch and lay down again, intending to take a short rest. But now the jet lag had me and my eyelids started to sink as if they were attached to counterweights at the bottom of a well. Within seconds I was almost asleep when I could hear Hodaka laugh and shout to the two girls. The shoji screen slid open and the girls giggled as they approached me. I felt some fingers caressing my sleeve, others fluttering by my pocket toward my groin.

"They want to read your future," said Hodaka.

Fine by me, I thought, as I heard my zipper open. My belt

was flicked open and my pants pulled down and I felt a pair of hands slide across the inside of my thigh. Another pair cradled my penis and gently lifted it upward for inspection as if it were a palm. Which was the lifeline, I wondered, and which the loveline? I wanted to watch but I was so tired my eyelids resisted any effort. It didn't seem to matter anyway. In a few seconds my penis hardened and my immediate future made any long-term predictions completely irrelevant.

The next thing I remember I was dreaming—a long, erotic dream that began with Sara and Toto cavorting in my bed and evolved into Laura Suzuki standing by a silvery mountain lake in a flowered silk kimono. She turned to me as I approached her. But then, just as we were about to touch, she drew a dagger from her sash and plunged it into my back like the beautiful siren in *Rashomon*. I awoke in a cold sweat beneath the quilt of a futon which had been spread across the floor near the sofa. It was pitch dark; the only thing illuminating the room was the golden glow of the blowfish coming from across the street.

I forced myself to go back to sleep and awoke the next morning to the sound of Hodaka talking on the phone.

"Ichikawa will meet us today," he said, hanging up. "At the inn at Mount Sadao."

"Where's that?" I sat up to see another attractive young woman I assumed to be Fumiko meticulously polishing the kitchen counter although the top itself already looked clean enough for a minor surgical procedure.

"About an hour from Tokyo. We will take Fumiko's car."

She has a car too, I thought. These Japanese men seemed to have everything under control. Somewhere, somehow, they had to pay for it.

I shaved and showered in the tiny bathroom behind the kitchen, balancing myself precariously so I wouldn't fall into the squat toilet. A half hour later I was riding with Hodaka in

Fumiko's Nissan President, heading for Mount Sadao. It was a fancier car than I had expected, the kind of Japanese car you don't see in the States but that I had noticed parked at the entrances of several larger office buildings in the Marunouchi District. The ones I'd seen were usually chauffeur-driven. I wondered how Fumiko had gotten it, whether she was the daughter of some rich family.

Hodaka didn't say much as we continued east along the motorway, parts of which were built right on the roofs of buildings themselves to save space. Tokyo was an endless city, like L.A., with no precise downtown, but soon we approached something approximating a suburban area. Mountains out of a brush painting loomed in the distance. Hodaka pointed out Mount Sadao and told me it was a haven for lovers. The restaurant itself where we were meeting Ichikawa was a famous assignation spot and built in the old style.

"It is odd for him to pick a place like that," Hodaka said. He appeared tense. "Do you think it is what you call a setup?"

"I doubt it. It would seem too suspicious. If you're going to set somebody up, why tip him off? Of course, you never know."

Hodaka looked relieved, but there was a sense of disappointment about him too, as if he had been deprived of his chance to be at the center of the action.

We turned off the motorway onto a winding mountain road. A local motorcycle gang roared past us as we continued around, curving into a wooded gorge that reminded me of places in northern New England like Franconia Notch. It was hard to believe we were only minutes from the outskirts of the world's second largest city.

A few seconds later we made a left onto a gravel road leading to the inn at Mount Sadao. A number of expensive cars—Mercedes, Jaguars, plus several of the more expensive Japanese sedans like the one we were in—were parked in a small lot opposite the inn building—the reconstruction of a *daimyo's* mansion from the late Tokugawa Period. Hodaka and I walked over a small bridge above a brook filled with dark gray *koi* to the steps of the entrance foyer, where we took off our shoes beneath an ancient scroll painting of a laughing monk. The temperature was in the low thirties and my feet shivered as I slid them into a pair of slippers and followed the hostess down a polished wood corridor. A wall of windows opened out onto a moss-filled interior garden with one stone lantern and a bonsai tree. This was Rigrod's Japan, I thought, momentarily flashing on his Zen garden with the image of Laura Suzuki seated in the lotus position, her bare chest to the setting California sun. I froze, hearing the retort of gunfire in my mind's ear. But it was only the sound of a shoji screen sliding open. Hodaka and I were motioned into a private dining room where not Ichikawa but a handsome silver-haired gentleman in a blue pinstripe Wall Street suit was sitting, cross-legged at the low dining table, drinking tea. He stood immediately and greeted us with a bow.

"Mr. Wine, I presume," he said in English with a slight Oxonian accent. "And Mr. Hodaka." He pronounced the translator's name with a slight disdain that implied a difference in rank as unbridgeable as the mountain pass above us. "I am Mr. Okakura."

"How do you do?" I said, extending my hand. Okakura shook it politely but perfunctorily. The Japanese did not enjoy the custom. I did not bother to ask about Ichikawa. He was the most obvious of intermediaries and I would have been surprised to have seen him there in the first place.

Okakura nodded for us to sit and clapped his hands for the waitress, who appeared immediately with a tray of hot towels and passed them around. "You must be hungry, Mr. Wine," said Okakura, wiping his face with his towel. "You have come a long way for a minor insurance adjustment."

"Every claim must be answered," I said. "And sometimes

they prove to be more important than they first appear."

"Yes, that is true. Sake, Mr. Wine?" He lifted the sake jar and poured some into my cup. "In Japan it is not considered proper to pour for ourselves." Then he poured some for Hodaka, who reciprocated in his. "So . . . you have come to satisfy a claim on an accident."

"Of sorts, yes. Although I'm not sure if it was an accident or deliberate."

"What seems to have occurred?"

"Some information belonging to my employer appears to have vanished."

Okakura nodded. Hodaka's eyes widened slightly.

"Information can be hard to find, Mr. Wine."

"Yes. In a sense it doesn't exist."

"Indeed." Okakura tilted slightly toward the window. Outside a water wheel was turning by another small bridge. Its slow, rhythmic creaks mingled with the mournful sound of an ancient stringed instrument coming from a hidden speaker. "It is the samisen," said Okakura. "And what sort of information was this, Mr. Wine?"

"To be perfectly frank, Mr. Okakura, I'm not sure. Technological information of a sort belonging to the—"

"Tulip Computer Corporation?"

"Yes."

Hodaka started in surprise just as a waitress entered, bringing us each a plate of raw white fish sliced so thin it was practically transparent.

"I hope you like sashimi," said Okakura.

"As long as it isn't blowfish."

Okakura smiled slightly. "Not blowfish, Mr. Wine. They do not serve that here. This is a rare freshwater sashimi from Lake Biwa. Taste it."

I tried the fish, which had an exquisite fineness about it, a light, almost airy quality like a melting candy that wasn't sweet.

"Truly excellent, Mr. Okakura. You can't find anything like this in the United States."

"I am certain not."

"Tell me, though"—I placed my chopsticks on a perfect little ceramic holder in the shape of a jumping frog— "as a lover of sushi, where would I be able to find some blowfish?"

"The kind you are after?"

I nodded.

"You might do better looking for that in California. I understand they have some excellent fresh fish there." He poured me another glass of sake as Hodaka filled his glass. "I do not believe it is available here . . . *kampai*." He emptied his sake.

"Oh, really . . . I was certain it was here."

"Mr. Wine, if it were here, it would already have been chewed up and digested, copied by our machines. There is no reason to waste your time. Go back to the Imperial Hotel and enjoy yourself. Try some of our nightclubs, visit the temples of Kyoto, then return to the United States. You are making a fool of yourself in our eyes chasing about cheap electronic shops with the author of *Madame O Goes to Dallas*." Hodaka blanched. "And you know what attention we Japanese pay to face."

"So I've heard, Okakura-san. Of course, I hope you feel the same way about agents of the GRU."

"Mr. Maximov—late of the San Francisco section? Representatives of Third World nations do not concern us."

"That's a rather large and powerful Third World nation."

"But Third World nevertheless. They would not understand a blowfish even if they had one in their hands."

"I suppose not. But they might know how to use it."

"To do what? Blow up Korean airliners that have accidentally strayed into their airspace? That could have been done by someone holding a bazooka in the basket of an open-air balloon." The waitress came in and took our empty plates, replacing them with small pieces of filet mignon grilling on individual molded-ceramic hibachis. "So relax, Mr. Wine. A Russian blowfish would be useless without a properly trained chef, and here in Japan"—he sliced himself a piece of beef—"it would be used for commercial purposes only—and in such a way, I can assure you, so as not to conflict with the immediate interests of the Tulip Computer Corporation."

"Who told you that—Laura Suzuki?"

Okakura dismissed this with a wave. "In the final analysis, they are doomed anyway."

"Tulip?"

"I will be perfectly honest with you, Mr. Wine. This economic rivalry is not a game to us. Ninety-five percent of our food and raw materials are imported. We do not have the luxury you do to become a second-rate agrarian society. We must grow industrially or die. Now, have a little Kobe beef. Even that will disappear in a few years as we clear out the grazing land to make way for new steel plants and semiconductor factories."

"I wouldn't want to interfere with progress," I said, taking a piece of the meat in my chopsticks and swallowing it. It was practically as tender as the raw fish.

"And please be kind enough to abandon this futile search of yours," he continued. "As you have no doubt noted, we are always fully apprised of your whereabouts. If you decide to persist, we will have no recourse but to inform your government that a private citizen is making illegal investigations on Japanese soil and to rescind your visa, which, I understand, was not obtained through the proper channels anyway."

The waitress entered and whispered something to Okakura, who nodded and stood. "You will have to excuse me now. I must attend to an emergency meeting. It was a pleasure to meet you, Mr. Wine . . . and Mr. Hodaka. Enjoy yourselves— there are twelve more courses, all paid for by the ministry."

"Which ministry is that?" I asked.

"The Ministry of International Trade and Industry." He bowed, handed me a card, and exited.

"A MITI man," said Hodaka, trying to sound casual about having been in the presence of one of the honchos of the organization that was said to have engineered Japan's Economic Miracle, but I could tell from the tremor in his voice that he was somewhat overawed.

"Maybe they'll put some export pressure on your books."

Hodaka forced a smile while trying to pick up some beef. But it slipped clumsily back onto the grill as if he were a foreigner struggling to use chopsticks for the first time.

We skipped most of the rest of the meal and headed back into the city before the rush-hour traffic. I wasn't sure what this MITI guy really wanted or even who he really was, but I decided not to take any chances and play the dutiful tourist for a while, so I had Hodaka take me back to the Imperial again.

"Are you still interested in a job?" I asked him as we drove past the Emperor's Palace, turning into the immense porte cochere of the hotel.

"Of course," he said. "The story is just beginning to get good."

"Great. Cut me in on some of the royalties. But remember, from here on in, your phone is likely to be tapped and so will mine. In fact, both of them probably already are. So if you want to reach me, dial my number once and hang up. Then I'll call you back on a pay phone at the fortune-telling studio ten minutes later."

Hodaka nodded and followed me into the hotel to get my room number while I checked in again.

"Ah, Mr. Wine," said the concierge. "How doing? We are so glad you check in again. We have message for you and we have no idea what to do with it." He handed me a carefully lettered envelope on hotel stationery. I opened it while Hodaka looked

up the number of the fortune-telling studio. It said CALL ME.
PLEASE. LAURA. 444-7451.

10

I SAT IN MY ROOM wondering whether it was a love letter or a
death warrant. In all probability it was neither, but those were
the only two possibilities that came immediately to mind. So I
marked time by sending a telegram to Wiz: NO LUCK. BACK
SOON AFTER A LITTLE TOKYO TOURISM. MOSES.

Then I went out and took a walk in the Ginza, past the Sony
Building and the Crystal Building and down to the Matsuya
Department Store and back again. The night was balmy for
April. Conservative businessmen, their ties slightly askew,
wobbled uncertainly from drink in the doorways of swank
nightclubs while being teased and flattered by the elegantly
dressed hostesses who hung on their every word like surrogate
mother-geishas. It was an odd system, almost perverse, but,
unlike L.A. or San Francisco, at least in Tokyo you could find a
decent heterosexual bar.

I stopped at a toy store to buy my kids some plastic Japanese
robot watches, even though I suspected they were already too
old for them. Coming out, I saw a pay phone, the bright red
kind that dot Japanese streets like brilliant stabs of lipstick in
the night. I was feeling lonely, that acute loneliness you feel in
a foreign country when you're by yourself and you have
nowhere to go and no one to talk to in the first place, so I

stared at the phone like a lifeline going nowhere. 444-7451, I thought. 444-7451—the numbers seemed so familiar to me, so American, as if I were calling my friend David to see if he wanted to go to the gym for a steam bath.

So I dropped in my ten-yen coin and dialed.

"*Moshi-moshi,*" came the voice on the other end.

"Hello. Do you speak English?"

There was some confusion on the other end, followed by the clunk of a phone being left on a table. I heard some back and forth in Japanese as I scanned the sidewalk to make sure no one was watching me. But how would I know? I was about to hang up when another voice came on the line.

"*Moshi-moshi!* May I help you please?"

"Yes. Who are you?"

"Rippa Rippa Tsurekomi."

"Rippa Rippa Tsurekomi? Is that a place or a person?"

"*Moshi-moshi?*"

"Where are you?"

"Excuse please." There was another clunk as the phone went down on the table again. I didn't want to ask for Laura directly and I had a suspicion my time was running out. I was sure it was running out when I noticed a man in a black shirt standing about fifty feet away in the stairwell of the Ginza subway station.

I hung up and walked casually in his direction, continuing directly past him without looking, and went down the steps to the first floor of the station, emerging in a large underground area about the size of a football field with numerous lines heading off in different directions. I chose the Ginza-Sen line at random, pushing through a crowd of pedestrians down a long corridor and picking up my speed. But it was to no avail. As soon as I reached a row of shops at the end of the corridor, I could see the black-shirted man a few yards behind me reflected in the polished window of a pachinko parlor. He was tall for a Japanese and wore a felt hat that tilted over his fore-head just above a crescent-shaped scar that looked as if it had been carved by an unfriendly sword or one of those bizarre weapons they sell in the back of martial arts magazines. Maybe I had gone soft from too much association with computer nerds, but whatever it was, he had survived it and I certainly didn't want to test him, especially here in a land where I didn't even have the slightest notion how to yell "Help, police!"

So I surveyed the row of underground shops, looking for a way out, or at least a place a Westerner might blend with the crowd. Then I saw a sign that said MAXIM'S DE PARIS. Could this be real, I thought, here in the Ginza subway station? I didn't waste time debating this, however, and followed the sign toward the end of the shops. It led past a subterranean garage into a cul-de-sac where Maxim's itself, a carbon copy of the original on the Rue Royale, curled in art nouveau splendor in the basement of the Sony Building.

I caught an uncomfortable flicker in the eye of my black-shirted pursuer as I entered with cock-hatted nonchalance, angled over to the posh velvet bar, and ordered a glass of Rémy Martin from the Japanese bartender, who looked incongruous in front of the ornate mirror straight out of Toulouse-Lautrec. The bar was filled with a crush of tourists, Japanese business-men, and what I guessed to be a demimonde of foreign resi-dents who hung around out of a combination of nostalgia and the opportunity to rub shoulders with those rich enough to pay the freight at the Tokyo branch of one of the world's most famous restaurants.

I chose a woman out of this latter group, a lonely-looking blonde about forty in a slightly frayed dress who was leaning against the far end of the bar, near where a Japanese pianist was playing a florid version of "La Vie en Rose," and walked over to her under the close scrutiny of Mr. Black Shirt.

"Hello, Denise, how've you been?" I said, coming up and

embracing her. The woman gave me a cockeyed look but I continued in a low voice before she could say anything. "Interested in a free dinner at Maxim's . . . no questions asked, no . . . quid pro quo—y'know what I mean?"

"I think so. Sure." She had a British accent.

"Denise, you're a sweetheart! This is gonna be a helluva night!" I replied brightly, taking her by the arm and escorting her right past the black shirt toward the dining room.

"Sandor Hathaway, reservation for two," I said to the maitre d', who looked down in confusion at his book. I smoothed the way with a ten-thousand-yen note and inside of a minute "Denise" and I were whisked through the entrance of the main dining salon to a banquette out of sight of my frustrated friend. Two minutes later, I slipped another ten thousand yen in Denise's purse and disappeared through the kitchen. It was an expensive getaway, but Wiz could afford it.

I jumped into a cab in front of the Sony Building and leaned over to the driver.

"Rippa Rippa Tsurekomi," I told him.

"*Wakaranai?*" He looked confused.

"Rippa Rippa Tsurekomi," I repeated.

"*Wakaranai?*"

I could see we weren't getting anywhere. I took out a pencil and paper and wrote the words down for him in block letters.

"Ahhh," he said. "Rippa Rippa Tsurekomi!"

"Right, just what *I* said."

He took off. About an hour and another thirty thousand yen later we were driving through the outskirts of the city again, this time, I think, in the northern suburbs.

"Rippa Rippa Tsurekomi?" I asked again, beginning to get more than a little insecure.

"*Hai, hai* . . . Rippa Rippa Tsurekomi." The driver nodded his head insistently. Who was I to argue?

Ten minutes later we pulled up at the gangplank of a large

neon-lit imitation boat about the size of a small ocean liner parked in the middle of a dirt lot. Flags and streamers were draped from the side and a giant heart fluttered from the mast. At first glance it seemed like one of those obnoxious "theme" restaurants you find in some of the more commercial areas of Orange County, but from the looks of the colored lights in some of the portholes, I had the sensation it was something else.

"Rippa Rippa Tsurekomi!" The driver pointed, urging me out of the cab after I paid a sum roughly the equivalent of a discount flight from Chicago to the Bahamas. I felt a twinge of anxiety as he took the money with a quick bow and disappeared into the night, leaving me standing alone next to an earthbound boat in an empty parking lot.

I climbed the gangplank and passed through the automatic electric-eye door and into a dimly lit entry chamber. A woman was sitting behind a glass booth reading a magazine. She paid no attention as I entered, and I looked from her to a panel of illuminated transparencies that occupied the wall opposite. Each one showed a room, presumably inside this "boat," with a price written underneath and a little red light to indicate, I assumed, whether it was occupied. The rooms themselves were tarted up in the manner of X-rated motels, but were far more posh than anything I had seen at home. Beyond the usual waterbeds, video equipment, and mirrored ceilings, each had its own fantasy theme from Thirties Hollywood to Early Shogun with consistent decor and elaborate baths, ranging from standard hot tubs to a giant pearlized clam shell built for two. Hodaka was right again—there were things in Tokyo you could never find in New York or L.A. . . . if, indeed, I was still in Tokyo.

"Moses, I'm so glad you've come."

I turned to see Laura standing behind me. Even in the half-light, I could sense something different about her. Her complexion was flushed and there was a burning intensity in her dark brown eyes I had never noticed before.

"Where are we, Laura?"

"Rippa Rippa Tsurekomi—Magnificent Magnificent Love Hotel. Not everything in Japan is paper folding and flower arrangement."

"So I've gathered. What's supposed to happen next? We go make love in one of the rooms and then I die of electrocution on a waterbed?"

"This place belongs to my aunt—the last surviving member of my family. It was the only place I could come."

"Why? You in trouble? You're in Japan now. You're all one big family here, haven't you heard?"

"That's what I thought, yes." She looked away. "Until I got off the plane."

"What happened to you then? Traffic jams too big? Or the smog? Or weren't they grateful enough? You didn't get the Hirohito Medal for bringing the plans to Blowfish."

"You should have the answer to that."

"*I* should? What kind of bullshit is that? I followed you half-way across the world!"

"Don't play innocent with me!"

"I never felt more innocent in my life, thank you." And I meant it.

"All right, Moses, if you insist." She half smiled and looked at me. "Come with me to my room. It is safer, near the back . . . and if anyone's following you, my aunt can warn us." She nodded toward the woman behind the window, who was staring at us now. She was in her late fifties and her skin was an ugly salmon color from her chin to her forehead, as if the entire right side of her face had been burned. "Come," said Laura. "And I will tell you who I am."

I followed her down a corridor past several rooms with closed doors—the sound of Sarah Vaughan doing "Lover" coming from one and Rod Stewart singing "Hot Legs" from another—

until we reached an imitation bulkhead at the end. Laura unlocked the hatch and we entered an art deco ocean liner suite as perfectly copied as the dining room at the Sony Maxim's with *moderne* lighting fixtures and geometric patterns of inlaid brass around the portholes.

"It is the exact replica of the bridal suite on the *Queen Elizabeth II*," said Laura. She leaned against the bar and looked at me. In the recessed lighting, I could see her better now. She wore a blue dress with a floral pattern and her thick hair was pinned up with a black lacquer comb, a white gardenia sprouting from the side. Her lips were painted a bright scarlet, as if someone had sliced a big sensual gash in the center of her mouth. "My name is Yasuko Tadao," she said. "I was born in Yokohama on June fourth, 1961."

Yokohama 1961? White gardenias? This wasn't the Laura I knew. This was some kind of high-tech Tokyo Rose.

"Hello . . . Yasuko?"

"Hello, Moses. Would you like to hear some music? There is a library of Cole Porter records to match the decor." Her eyes danced with a strange irony, as if she were enacting a role for my benefit, just as before she had enacted her California role.

"How about a white dinner jacket for me and an ermine shawl for your gorgeous shoulders? No thanks, Yasuko. I'm not in the mood for music right now. Or for acting out some romantic foreplay à la Noël Coward. I need to know why you brought me here—and what this is all about."

"I want you to tell me what happened to Blowfish."

"You what?"

"You saw me get on that plane. The minute I got off, it was taken from me. You obviously notified someone, who was waiting on the other end."

"That's ridiculous. First of all, I wasn't sure you had it. Secondly, I didn't know anybody here to pick it up if I was.

And third of all, if I already had it, why wouldn't I already be on a plane home instead of burning up company money at the Imperial Hotel?"

"Yes, you do work for Tulip, don't you?" She shook her head. "That's no surprise to you."

"Activists . . . idealists. You're all the same—hypocrites."

"*I'm* the hypocrite?"

"The private eye who fought political corruption, defended the poor." She half smiled, walking toward me. "I can't believe you're working for a corporation."

"That corporation gave me a job and helped me put my life back together. Before that, I was sitting around in my bathrobe, staring at the walls."

"And for that you sold out everything you stood for?"

"Oh, come on, Yasuko. This is the real world. You can't sit in a closet dreaming all your life. Besides, it's interesting work. I like having a little responsibility for a change." I stopped and looked at her, still unable to digest this amazing switch in identity. "So if Blowfish *was* stolen from you," I continued, "who do you think took it?"

"I don't know." She smiled seductively.

"Well, who were you working for?"

"That's not important now." She waved. "I have been deceived." She smiled again and touched my cheek. "You sure you don't want to listen to Cole Porter?"

"I thought you were going to tell me who you were."

"Later," she said, walking over to the turntable and switching it on. Ella Fitzgerald singing "Easy to Love" insinuated its way through a pair of hidden speakers with a clarity the original passengers on the *Queen Elizabeth II* could only have dreamed of. I listened to the song for a moment. It had always been one of my favorites—seemingly light, but actually dark and almost torturedly romantic, a song of unrequited love written by a homosexual in an era when few had the courage to proclaim it.

I looked at Yasuko. Why did I remain so attracted to her? Because she was exotic, because she was dangerous, because there was a gulf between us so wide I would never, finally, be called upon to reveal myself? It was the fascination with the mysterious that at once propelled my professional and romantic lives and kept me removed from both—an outsider, always an outsider.

Yasuko approached and we began to dance on the parquet floor of the suite. She moved gracefully and I turned her, catching our reflection in the mirror. I felt like we were in a time capsule. It could've been the late thirties. Japan was in Manchuria, the U.S. moving westward, entrenching its positions in Guam and the Solomons. Pearl Harbor was around the corner. And then, and then . . .

We continued dancing as she dropped her head onto my shoulder. I reached down, sliding my hand across the back of her dress. She wore a thin silk fabric that made her almost naked to the touch. Her neck smelled of a perfume resembling frangipani, dense and erotic. She stroked my shoulders and, edging her thigh between mine, moved us slowly toward the bed.

"I'll show you something different. Something they only do in the Orient," she whispered in my ear.

I smiled. "Sounds interesting."

She laughed softly. "You've seen the old prints. Sometimes we do it with our clothes on . . . and sometimes with these." She opened a drawer to reveal an amazing array of sexual apparatus—unguents, dildos, restraints, nipple clips, ticklers, and strange devices whose uses I could only guess at. She took out a butt plug and a shiny pair of ben-wa balls, unfastened a clip that allowed a portion of her skirt to flop open, and slid the balls into her vagina. Then she pulled down my zipper. We rolled over onto the bed, her pants slipping down only slightly and her dress draping over me like a quilt. I ran my tongue across her naked stomach as she spread-eagled me at the crouch and, leaning over, pushed the butt plug into my anus. Fabric brushed against my skin, a shock wave of sensation running up my anal cavity toward the prostate. I held her thighs, sucking on her breast as she reached up and removed a long pointed object from her hair, holding it in the air and bending it backward as if she were about to plunge it in my back. Suddenly realizing what was happening, I bolted upward, grabbing her wrist and twisting it. Surprisingly strong, she resisted, but I kept pulling until the object—a knife— grazed my chest and clattered to the floor. Then I rolled over on top of her, pushing my knees into her shoulders and pinning her to the bed. For a split second she looked at me with utter contempt, then pursed her lips and spat in my face.

"Americans are all the same!"

"Yeah, right, like Japanese," I said. "The Yellow Peril."

"What do you know!"

"I wasn't trying to kill you here, lady." I grabbed her wrist again and twisted. "All right, I'll ask you again. Who took Blowfish?"

"Fuck you!"

I twisted harder. "You want more? You want it all the way off? Don't think I won't do it. As far as I'm concerned, chivalry died two seconds ago!" I turned her another ten degrees.

"All right. All right. It doesn't make any difference anyway. It was a man in a black shirt."

"With a scar?"

"How do you know?"

"Just guessed. And who are you working for?" I applied another degree of pressure.

"Mita Kokusai. They are cowards."

"Who's Mita Kokusai?"

"The Japanese government."

"The Japanese government is paying assassins to knife innocent Americans?"

"They should kill *all* Americans!"

"Oh, terrific. And just what is Blowfish?"

I was waiting for an answer when I felt the cold steel of a gun barrel in the small of my back.

Yasuko looked at me and smiled. "Get up now, Moses."

I turned around slowly to see her aunt standing behind me, both hands clutching a shotgun. Yasuko slipped out quickly from underneath me.

"Moses Wine, this is my aunt Akiko. She also has a great distaste for Americans."

"Evidently."

I looked from the older woman, who, at close range, appeared even more disfigured by hideous red scar tissue, to Yasuko, who was staring at me with a hatred intense enough to melt the thicker regions of the polar cap.

"Fortunately she was behind the building when it happened. My poor parents were not so lucky."

"Before what happened?"

"Don't make me laugh." She reached down and picked up the knife. "Good-bye, Moses. There's no way I can let you free to find Blowfish. And let me assure you, if I had any idea what it was or where it was, I would not give you the slightest clue."

She turned toward me with the knife.

Immediately I spun around, grabbed the barrel of the shotgun, and pushed away as it went off in my hands, spraying shot into the art deco mirror and sending peach glass flying in every direction. Just managing to hang on to the gun, I wrested it from Aunt Akiko and swung it around, knocking the knife from Yasuko's hand with the butt. People were screaming from several rooms, banging on walls.

Grabbing my clothes and dressing as I ran, I raced out of the room, down the corridor past several terrified patrons, and then down the gangplank of the love hotel out into the night. I didn't stop until I was across the parking lot and down the other side of an alley into the next street. Not a soul was about.

It wasn't for a couple of minutes—when a passing car abruptly sped up as it passed me—that I realized I was casually walking along carrying a shotgun. I quickly shoved it under a nearby pickup truck and continued on, walking in the direction I assumed to be south. After about fifteen minutes I came to a more urban area, a scattering of neon signs still blinking forlornly. One of them read CAPSULE HOTEL in English and Japanese. A couple of Japanese guys—young corporate types in the ubiquitous blue suits—were carrying a buddy toward it who was singing at the top of his lungs and looking considerably more than three sheets to the wind. My adrenaline supply suddenly felt completely depleted. I stood and watched as their friend bent over and blew his lunch right there on the sidewalk. Nobody seemed embarrassed. They grinned and waved to me, pointing toward the hotel, which looked like some kind of way station for wayward executives who couldn't make it home for the night, probably some of the same guys I had seen flirting with their hostess–girl friends at the Ginza bars earlier that evening. Checking my watch, I realized that the subways had been closed for nearly an hour, so I half walked, half stumbled in after them and headed up to the clerk, digging into my pocket and forking over a few thousand flaccid yen. He handed me a key to my capsule and pointed up the stairs. The room itself, which was entered by a ladder and only about four feet high by seven feet long, was a capsule indeed, a sarcophagus for the living. But inside it was clean as a hospital with all the conveniences of modern Japan, from videocassette to laser disk to microprocessor-controlled beverages and snacks all exquisitely arranged in one tiny container. Not that I gave a damn. I was too exhausted even to flick a switch.

11

I AWOKE THE NEXT DAY at ten and phoned Hodaka, letting it ring once and then calling back five minutes later at the fortune-telling joint. He picked up immediately.

"*Moshi-moshi.*"

"*Moshi-moshi* yourself. This is Moses."

"I know. Where have you been? I have been trying to reach you. We would like you to lecture tonight."

"Lecture!"

"Yes. To the Maltese Falcon Society. It is an organization of fans of the mystery novel. We often have guest lecturers, but you would be the first real American private eye."

"Sounds fascinating. Bet you even serve tea."

"Johnny Walker Black Label."

"Better and better. Look, what's Mita Kokusai?"

"It's an office building—near the Shiba Park."

"Great. Meet me there in forty-five minutes."

I hung up and headed for the nearest subway station. It turned out to be the northernmost stop on the Chiyoda line and it was a long haul—including a transfer—all the way down to Shiba Koen, the nearest stop to the park. It was another ten minutes to the Mita Kokusai Building and I was five minutes late when I arrived. Hodaka was waiting for me in the lobby, looking rather pleased with himself.

"Someone was watching my building but I gave him the slip through the pachinko parlor next door."

"Terrific," I said. "Maybe you should give the lecture." I walked over to the building directory and started to look through it. I was about to call Hodaka over, but it turned out that no translation was necessary. Among all the businesses on the twenty-three floors of the building, one of them was listed in English and it jumped right out at me—Institute for New Generation Computer Technology—ICOT. Back in the Silicon Valley I must have heard it mentioned a dozen times. It was the most famous computer experiment in Japan, written up in *Time, Newsweek, InfoWorld,* and, I imagined, numerous other periodicals I didn't read or couldn't understand. Forty brilliant young engineers—forty samurai—had been brought from all over their country to create a new computer for the 1990s, a fifth generation of computer to generate that new wealth of nations—information. It was to be a machine that could think and infer as sophisticatedly as any human, only a thousand, maybe a million, times faster. And they, the Japanese, were going to build this all by themselves, bigger and better than their older brother, their former occupying power—us. I remembered the words of "Cassiopeia"—"Use your artificial intelligence"—and turned to Hodaka. "We're going to the twenty-first floor," I told him.

The Japanese certainly didn't go in for ostentation. For such an ambitious undertaking, the offices of ICOT—two large rooms with desks and computer terminals and a couple of small offices in the back for the head honchos—made Tulip look like a combination of Universal Studios and an expensive health spa. I immediately identified myself to the receptionist, who passed me over with equal rapidity to their public relations director, a pinch-faced young woman at a desk only fifteen feet away. Leading Hodaka and me over to a sitting area, she identified herself as Mitsuko Ezawa, an engineering graduate of the University of Oregon.

"We admire Tulip very much," she said. "Can we get you some tea?"

"That won't be necessary. Look, uh, Miss Ezawa, I would like to speak with your director."

"Mr. Kimura is busy today. I am sorry. Perhaps I can help you."

"No offense, ma'am, but unless you want a serious international incident on your hands, I think you better get Mr. Kimura over here on the quick."

Miss Ezawa reddened, embarrassed by my American abruptness.

"I do not understand."

"I have reason to believe your institute has stolen or attempted to steal proprietary ideas of the Tulip Computer Corporation and either directly or indirectly caused the murder of two persons, one an American national and one a Taiwanese national."

In two minutes we were sitting in the office of Mr. Kimura with the door shut behind us, Kimura rattling away in Japanese to Miss Ezawa. He was young for a Japanese director, hardly over forty, and dressed with the studied casualness of the old Kennedy crew, rolled sleeves and Adidas tennis sneakers. A photograph of him on a mountaineering expedition was pinned to the bulletin board behind him with a series of printouts.

"Mr. Kimura says what you are implying is patently ridiculous," Ezawa translated. "Tulip is a personal computer corporation whose work bears little relation to ICOT, which is a research institute in the process of designing a large sequential inference machine many times that size."

I glanced over at Hodaka, who confirmed the translation.

"The Bulb computer is pretty sophisticated."

Kimura smiled before it was repeated in Japanese, then said something to Ezawa. I was reminded of what I had read about Zhou Enlai, how he spoke several languages fluently but would never speak except through an interpreter. "Mr. Kimura says he has never seen the Bulb computer but imagines it is a nice little machine for playing games and doing income taxes. However, the only organizations in your country whose work would be of interest to him would be the military and GTI."

So much for the Wiz's great garage revolution of computer youth. I made a note to tell Giles Brisbane to revise his debate next time I saw him. Then I looked at Kimura. The man was disturbed about something, something he wasn't sure he wanted to hold back. Instead of prodding him, I waited for him to speak. At length he turned to Hodaka this time and began talking in a far more halting, less expansive manner.

"Mr. Kimura wonders if you know a woman who came to see him yesterday."

"Yasuko Tadao."

Kimura nodded. He waited again before continuing to talk to Hodaka. "She seemed to think she was working for him," said the mystery writer. Miss Ezawa looked concerned, as if her boss were revealing too much.

"She was an employee of Tulip under the name of Laura Suzuki."

Kimura frowned. "I must make phone call," he said, suddenly in English.

"Please don't. I think it's best for both of us if we continue this conversation confidentially."

Kimura thought for a second, then told Ezawa and Hodaka to leave. When they were gone, I told him he spoke English very well.

"Not well," he said. "But I must know. You Americans afraid of us, but everything about computer written in English still. I must read information. Talk not so good."

"Good enough," I said. "A lot better than my Japanese." Or anybody's I knew, for that matter. "Did Miss Tadao have information she wanted to give you?"

"She said was stolen by her . . . from her?"

"From her. Do you have any idea what this information was?"

"Disk with source code for inference software."

"Inference software? I'm not sure what that is. It doesn't have anything to do with the Bulb, does it? Not an add-on or anything?"

"Bulb computer?" He laughed. "Oh no, no. I tell you—Bulb good machine. Make pretty pictures. I see in magazine. This all different."

Now I was getting confused. Wiz had said Blowfish was a Bulb computer add-on and this man was treating the Bulb like some toy for schoolchildren.

"You interested in Bulb—go Sanyo, go Sony. They make those kind things. That business. This institute of study. For future."

Future of what, I wondered? Obviously it wasn't all as peaches and cream as he wanted to make it sound, but it was clear that ICOT had bigger fish to fry than the personal computer market.

"So what's inference software?"

"Thinks. Does syllogisms. You know what is?"

"All men have ears. John is a man. Therefore John has ears."

"Right. That syllogism. We build machine does many syllogism. All at same time. Just like person . . . bing, bing, bing . . . but don't make mistake."

"And you're sure Yasuko Tadao wasn't working for you?"

"I know who working for me. Forty person. We not spies. We scientists." He stared at me with an expression that bordered on the haughty. "We don't need spy. We be there first anyway."

"Uh-huh." I glanced back at the photograph of him on the bulletin board. He was on the top of the mountain, waving a flag. But this was no Mount Fuji or even the High Sierras—it was Himalayan size. Maybe even Everest. This guy didn't kid around. "Listen, any idea why she thought she was working for you?"

"I not know." He half smiled. "She strange. She no like America much."

"Yeah, but . . . I still don't get it. She must have had some contact. Someone she thought was you."

He shook his head. "I not ask. I think she crazy."

He might have had a point there. I didn't have anything else to ask Kimura, but as an afterthought I remembered Eddie Capshaw's strange allegations about Rigrod working for the Japanese, so I confronted him bluntly: "Have you ever heard of an American computer scientist named Danny Rigrod?"

"Rigrod?" he replied distractedly. "Who that?" It didn't sound like he was lying.

I had a keen sensation of the limits of my own mind as I walked north along Shiba Park with Hodaka a few minutes later. The Tokyo Tower, an ersatz version of its cousin in Paris, loomed off to our right; the Azabu District, "where the rich people live," according to Hodaka, to our left; although, like everything in this city, you couldn't tell by looking. It was an external metaphor of my mind where, in its not so deep recesses, an impregnable steel wall had descended like a shield blocking me from insight or, more exactly, from its corollary, simple reality. Was Yasuko/Laura merely a dupe? And if so, why and for whom? And what was stolen from Tulip and when? Or was it nothing? Was I in pursuit of air—phantom signals of computer-generated energy dissipated into naught by the facile fingers of some precocious programmer? Ignorance was not bliss.

My only lead was a dangerous one, but I had no choice other than to follow it through. I led Hodaka into an atmospheric-looking coffee shop on the next corner, found the red telephone, and dialed the number of Chrysanthemum Computers in Akihabara that the clerk had given me on his card. Jazz was coming from an elaborate stereo—the old Miles Davis *Kind of Blue* album—and I hummed along to it until I connected, cutting straight through the usual round of *moshi-moshi*'s and getting right down to it.

"Hiya. I'm the American who wanted to buy your Bulb computer. I was going to look at it."

"Very good . . . very good. We fix . . . we fix."

"Where do I go? Back to your place in Akihabara?"

"No, no. Not Akihabara. Go TACT."

"TACT?"

"Tokyo . . . Air . . . Cargo . . . Terminal."

"You mean the airport?"

"No, no. Different place. Go TACT. Gate centy-cee."

"Centy-cee?"

"Yes. Centy-two, centy-cee. Ask Mr. Moritani."

"Tokyo Air Cargo Terminal. TACT. Gate twenty-three. Mr. Moritani."

"*Hai, hai.* Very good. You go now?"

"How long does it take?"

"Maybe ninety minute."

"Ninety minutes, huh?" I glanced over at Hodaka. "I'll leave in about an hour."

"*Hai, hai.* Very good . . . one hour."

I said good-bye and hung up, turning to Hodaka. "You got a gun?" I asked.

"Hjunnh . . . no." The detective writer looked distressed.

"We better find one—or I might not be back to address the Maltese Falcon Society tonight."

"Gun hard to find in Tokyo."

"Yeah. Right. You guys are nonviolent . . . when you're not lopping off heads with samurai swords or machine-gunning Manchurians."

"Ah, now great liberal makes nationalistic slurs."

"Just get us a gun, Hodaka. And Fumiko's car. And fast—so

we can get out there before they're ready. Otherwise we're walking into a setup so obvious it wouldn't even play on episodic television."

"Ah, a setup," said Hodaka, nodding, impressed by the real use of the genre term which, no doubt, he had translated many times.

"Yeah, I'm beginning to think this whole thing is a setup . . . a setup on a setup on a setup. But I'll explain it all at the meeting tonight, if you just cooperate. Now!"

"Yes, yes, Mr. Marlowe. I do it. I do it."

Twenty minutes later Fumiko's Nissan President pulled up in front of the coffee shop with a short, bald-headed man at the wheel who looked like his body was constructed out of ball bearings and thirty-gauge steel cable.

"This is Uno," said Hodaka, introducing the man, who instantly jumped out of the car and bowed to us. "I thought he might be useful. He is black belt in aikido, two times champion of the Miyagi Prefecture."

"*Ichiban . . . ichiban*," said Uno, continuing to bow to us, bobbing up and down like one of those miniature oil derricks along the San Bernadino Freeway.

"He is also technical adviser for the Maltese Falcon Society," Hodaka added, "so mystery writers may be accurate in their portrayals. He has great collection of weapons, both historical and contemporary, including *ninja* throwing disks and Russian Khlestakov AV-47 which are now in trunk of Nissan President."

"Great," I said as Uno continued to *ichiban*, holding the door for me as if I were some feudal lord. AK-47's? All I had wanted was one lousy pistol to keep in my pocket just in case. But I guess there was nothing like being prepared.

We drove the ninety minutes out to the Tokyo Air Cargo Terminal in Chiba-ken hardly saying a word to each other. The Japanese weren't long on small talk. "Silence is best"—I kept remembering what it said in *The Hagakure*. Shut up unless you've got something to say. I had a few relatives who could've benefited from that advice.

Hodaka broke the silence once to point out the Ministry of Justice and then the bland MITI building—the Ministry of International Trade and Industry—whose supposed representative had entertained us so lavishly at Mount Sadao. And then we hit the freeway heading south through industrial badlands so vast and polluted they made L.A. look like a national park for bird watchers.

We reached the air cargo terminal about a half hour before the appointed time and I had Hodaka park on the outskirts of the main lot hidden among some larger trucks. Uno said some words to him as we got out and Hodaka turned to me. "He wants to know if you want the AK-47 now."

"No, no. Not now. Something smaller would be fine."

Hodaka relayed my message to Uno, who opened the trunk and handed me a small Smith & Wesson revolver which I tucked under my jacket, remembering that I hadn't even fired a gun in target practice for two years and nowhere near a human being for about ten. Uno slid some sort of narrow dagger in his belt and palmed what looked like a poison dart straight from the Congo. There was something faintly ridiculous about the whole thing, carousing about the city famed for the lowest murder rate in the world with enough weaponry to launch a guerrilla war in a small Central American republic. But then it could've been just another example of Japanese hospitality. I was, after all, the honored guest and I *had* asked for protection.

We proceeded across the lot, past huge crates of electronic equipment, toward the loading gates, Uno and I in front and Hodaka stumbling a few feet behind looking about as pleased with the situation as a spurned lover at his girl friend's wedding. We passed several gates but twenty-three was nowhere in evidence until I saw it, all by itself, behind a chain-link fence at the far side of the lot. No one appeared to be around. A Toyota sedan with black windows sat out front next to a Lincoln Continental.

"Bring the car over there," I said to Hodaka, pointing toward a driveway about a hundred feet beyond the gate. The translator started off eagerly. Uno and I continued toward the loading gate. A small, one-story building stood just inside it with the names IWA IMPORTS and CHRYSANTHEMUM COMPUTERS in Japanese and English on the door. We were about to cross through when I heard noise coming from the back of the building. With the instincts of a cat burglar, Uno jumped back behind a massive shipping crate. I was right with him.

We watched as five men emerged from the building—the scarred man in the black shirt, a chauffeur, two nasty-looking gunsels out of a *yakuza* movie, and Mr. Okakura . . . the supposed MITI man. He stopped and gave some instructions to the gunsels, who turned and walked back into the building, where, I assumed, they would quietly polish their *katana* while awaiting my arrival. Then the chauffeur opened the door for Okakura, who got into the back seat of the Continental. My friend in the black shirt got into the front next to the chauffeur.

In a moment they were driving off. I didn't have to say a word to Uno, who immediately followed me over to the driveway where we awaited Hodaka in Fumiko's President. He arrived in about thirty seconds, just as the Continental was disappearing from sight beneath a freeway underpass.

"Follow that car!" I told him, pointing after it as I jumped in beside him.

"Aha, follow that car. . . . Right, gumshoe. Right!" said Hodaka, so delighted with the cliché that he forgot to be frightened. Uno clambered aboard in the back and we wheeled out, speeding through the underpass just in time to catch a glimpse of the Continental winding up onto the motorway back in the direction of Tokyo. "*Kuromaku*," said Hodaka. "That Okakura is black curtain man. I am sure."

We turned after him and headed north back into the big city. In a few minutes we were jammed up in a line of cars that made the Long Island Expressway look like a country road in Alaska. Tailing someone in Tokyo traffic was about as much fun as pulling wings off a gnat, but Hodaka seemed to be enjoying himself, staying close enough to keep an eye on the Continental while far enough back to remain a semi-indistinguishable blur in their rearview mirror. It wasn't a simple matter, but it was sure as hell boring to watch. I occupied myself counting the reproductions of Seiko Matsuda, the twenty-year-old wind-up doll whose last sixteen songs were the number-one best sellers in Japan. Her music was as original as strawberry Jell-O and her look so squeaky-clean and antiseptic that her billboards looked like diaper-service advertisements. Coming from the world of Boy George and Heavy Metal, she was the strangest thing I had seen in this country yet.

"He goes to station," said Hodaka as the Continental turned off on Sotobori-dori. He was clearly right. I could see the mammoth Tokyo Railroad Station straight ahead of us, a crush of cabs darting for it like lemmings toward a cliff. "What do I do with car?"

"Park it," I said.

Hodaka groaned anxiously and pulled the President into a hack stand on the east side of the station. We left it dangling there uneasily and followed Okakura & Co. into the building. I let Hodaka and Uno go several yards ahead of me, endeavoring to keep my white face as inconspicuous as possible in the yellow crowd. It was like trying to hide a ketchup bottle in a bag of marshmallows. Twice the man in the black shirt glanced behind him in the bodyguard's reflex to make certain they weren't being tracked. Both times I averted my head, ducking unceremoniously behind groups of Orientals who regarded me curiously, once bumping my head on a set of Rossignol skis in the hands of a student on his way to some mountain resort. So I allowed even more space between Hodaka and Uno before following them up the stairs. The mystery writer was waiting for me at the next landing.

"*Shinkansen*," he said, pointing ahead toward the second track. "They're taking the bullet train. It leaves in eight minutes!"

"Get tickets!" I said, thrusting a wad of yen in his hands.

"I don't know if that is enough," he said.

Jesus, I thought, digging into my other pocket and handing him whatever I had left, I was going to have one hell of an expense report for Wiz when I got back.

Ten minutes later I was sitting in car seven of the cream-and-blue bullet train, headed for Kyoto. Hodaka was beside me, Uno one row behind. Okakura, his chauffeur, and the black-shirted man were several cars back in car number eleven, first class. Feeling good, I stretched my legs and gazed through the window. From this perspective, it was hard to believe we were moving at a hundred and thirty miles per hour. Hodaka, too, was delighted with himself, looking around like a kid. He had just managed to phone Fumiko before he got on the train, informing her of the location of her car and postponing the meeting of the Maltese Falcon Society for a night.

It was already late afternoon and soon we were looking out to our right as the sun set over Mount Fuji. It was an impressive sight, even through the smog and the dense netting of telephone wires that crisscrossed the foreground like a thousand spiderwebs. I was just beginning to feel like a tourist when I felt the precise fingers of Uno tapping on my shoulder. I turned as he nodded behind him at the black-shirted man, who was entering our car through the rear door.

He had already seen me and I had no choice but to stand and start walking toward the front of the train. I pressed the automatic opener and headed into the next car, which had a long corridor leading to a snack counter. A lone attendant stood by a stack of carefully prepared box lunches of rice and seaweed. I lingered by him for a split second, then continued around the corner, spotted the door to the men's room, and entered.

It was a Japanese-style toilet with a hole in the floor and a pull chain up above. I deliberately left the door open a crack, slid my hand in my jacket, and waited. In a couple of moments the black-shirted man was at the door. He entered immediately, but before he could do anything, I slammed the door shut behind him and pulled the gun. My intention was to spin him around and land him a quick one on the back of the neck, but when I grabbed his arm, he jumped back and threw both his feet in the air, kicking outward and sending the gun rocketing into the window. I lunged at him, holding on to his arms and wrestling him into the wall, sliding on the floor, which had been swabbed with disinfectant. The train roared into a tunnel, a siren screaming into the darkness. Behind my head, I heard the flick of a knife like a stiletto coming out of its pocket. I pushed back at him, slamming my elbow into his gut, and brought my knee up to his groin. But he jumped back just in time and lifted his arm over his head. I could see the glinting blade reflected in the window. Acting instantly, I rolled to my side, lifting my leg outward, and kicked him as hard as I could in the kidneys.

"*Kutabare!*" he shouted—*Fuck you!*—as the knife skittered across the floor. I reached for it but the man suddenly slammed me across the shoulders with a vicious karate chop. I nearly blacked out and went careening into the wall, clinging to the toilet chain to stay erect and watching dizzily as he grabbed the gun this time and pointed it at me.

"*Gaijin sayonara,*" he said, squeezing the trigger. I struggled to react but dots swirled in front of my eyes, a shooting pain racing straight up my spinal column. I was about to kiss my ass good-bye when I heard the sharp grating sound of a zipper.

Only it wasn't a pair of pants opening—it was the black-shirted man's back. He crumpled to the floor in a pool of blood, sliced practically in two like a gutted fish from the shoulder blades to the tip of the coccyx. I looked up to see Uno standing behind him, sheathing a tiny crescent-shaped blade about the size of a penknife. He locked the door behind us and bowed.

"*Domo,*" I said, and picked up my gun.

"*Domo arigato gozaimasu,*" he replied, bowing again. Then he turned a faucet handle and started washing the black-shirted man's blood down the drain. It was a gruesome sight. After a few moments he signaled for me to leave.

I walked out into the corridor, wondering how he would dispose of the body. We were approaching Nagoya, another industrial city of several million. The train slowed and we passed another parade of billboards for Sony, Hitachi, and the rest as I continued down the car to where Hodaka was waiting for me.

"He's dead," I said quietly.

"Black Shirt?"

I nodded, taking my seat.

"Hjunnh," said Hodaka, brooding and frowning. "They will come looking for him."

"That's right."

We pulled to a halt at Nagoya Station. I figured it was about ten minutes before Okakura sent his chauffeur to look for the bodyguard. Fortunately the chauffeur had not been with us at the restaurant and would not recognize Hodaka or me. Of course, if Okakura went himself . . .

Three minutes later the train moved out again, precisely on schedule, continuing through the Kinki District to the ancient capital. In a short while the door opened and the chauffeur came through. Hodaka and I buried ourselves in the complimentary *shinkansen* magazine as he passed. I looked up at the last moment to see him exiting the far door just as Uno entered, coming the other way, followed by a family of French tourists. Uno nodded politely and took his seat without even looking at us. Several minutes later the chauffeur reappeared, coming back in the other direction, a puzzled frown on his face. He would report, I hoped, that their friend had betrayed them and slipped off in Nagoya. The problem was, in this country, from what I could tell, there weren't too many betrayals.

It was already dark when we arrived in Kyoto. Hodaka and I followed Uno off the train, first walking through several cars in order to disembark far to the front of Okakura and his man. When we reached the platform, Okakura was already walking toward the exit stairs with his chauffeur and a man in a rust-colored cloak. "Aha, a monk!" said Hodaka. "In Kyoto they say 'Throw a stone and one chance in two you will hit a student or a monk.'"

We followed the three of them down the stairs to the loading zone, where the monk ushered Okakura and his man into a waiting, chauffeur-driven Mercedes. Uno and I watched them pull out while Hodaka secured a cab. The driver already had his instructions when we got in, but was surprised to find an American in their party. In my own way, I was puzzled by the same thing. Why were they helping me, a foreigner working for a foreign corporation? It didn't fit with the blindly loyal kamikaze image we had of the Japanese.

Kyoto was a relatively small city and we left the dense high-rise area almost immediately, following the Mercedes through narrow, picturesque streets lined with old wood-frame buildings around garden courtyards, the Japan of another era. Hodaka repeatedly had to warn the driver not to come too close, but because of the complicated twists and turns, several times we nearly came abreast of the other car. They didn't appear to notice us, however, but continued on to a hillier part of the city as we passed a lantern-lit canal, cherry blossom petals floating on the water. Halfway up, the Mercedes turned into a gate of what looked, in the moonlight, to be a temple or shrine of some sort.

"Hjunnh," said Hodaka, making his sound of disturbance. He tapped the driver on the shoulder, indicating for him to pull over. "Is Daitoku-ji," he said to me. "National shrine of Soto Zen sect."

"Zen?" I repeated, interested in the magic word that had piqued my curiosity ever since I was a boy beatnik.

"Ach." Hodaka looked disgusted. "Americans, you all want to be Zen Buddhists. You think it is a hobby."

I paid the driver and we got out of the cab a couple of blocks from the shrine. Even in the dark I could tell it was a large complex, a couple of dozen buildings fanning out from the main gate of the temple.

We proceeded up the blocks and crossed through the main gate. Hodaka was puzzled that it was open at this time of night. Indeed it was strange that although the large wood doors to the complex were ajar, most of the buildings were dark. I glanced at the signs, one of which pointed toward the *honbo,* or abbot's quarters, another to the *butsuden,* or main hall, with, it said, a historical image of Sakyamuni Buddha himself. To my right was a storehouse of scriptures and beyond that, a belfry. Everything had the spare, almost severe aesthetic of disciplined tranquillity.

I heard the solemn boom of a temple gong, then the sound of feet shuffling along gravel. Meditation time, I thought, trying to follow the direction of some fleeting figures I saw scurrying through the night, but they disappeared into the darkness of a bamboo grove.

We continued on along a path of stone lanterns, passing by several temples and gardens. A teahouse stood to our left, the full moon casting a beam of diffused light through a high window on a small stone fireplace in its center. I heard a boisterous crack of laughter and then another, almost as loud as thunder. Hodaka, Uno, and I turned to see a bright illumination coming from one of the temples. A van was parked in front with a couple of cars. We headed toward it, the intensity of the light growing as we approached, coupled with the sound of some people clapping and more laughter, that same loud, cackling, thunderous laughter. On the side of the van I could read English letters. They said BBC. Through the narrow temple gate, a white face was visible, holding a video camera. I smiled. This was like Aunt Sonya all over again. I had arrived in the middle of a filming.

We walked through the gate, where indeed a crew of British documentarians were grouped around a monk who was sitting on a straw mat in between them mixing tea. He was big for a Japanese, with thick eyebrows and a high, furrowed forehead that pushed back almost endlessly to a large, shaved head like Erich von Stroheim's. He looked up when he saw us, pointing and grinning. I recognized immediately where the laughter had been coming from.

"Aha," he said. "More English and some of my countrymen. Welcome, welcome . . . have tea with us. *Cha-no-yu*—the great ceremonial tea of Japan. Zenism and teaism are greatly related. Indeed, Sen-no-Rikyu, the Father of the Tea Ceremony, prepared tea in this very room for Hideyoshi, the famous dictator-general of Japan. I bet you did not know that, yes?"

He was looking straight at me. "No, I didn't know that," I said.

"Aha, American! You are American!" He started laughing unrestrainedly. "Listen to this, American: 'Lightning flashes,/ Sparks shower./ In one blink of your eyes/ You have missed seeing.' That is Zen wisdom, yes?"

"Sounds like it."

"Sounds like it? I should know, should I not? I am *Roshi*

Kokaju, abbot of Daisen-in, subject of documentary on British television." He nodded from the film crew to the wall of the gift shop next door where, I could see, there were several poster-size photos of the abbot for sale, doing everything from raking the pebbles in the garden to appearing on a Japanese talk show before a studio audience of several hundred. "As you can see, I am no stranger to modern media. Also I am now running for office, running for what we call the Diet. So I am on a *political* diet—one part lies, two parts greed, and three parts corruption!" He grinned again, quite pleased with himself. "So, sit down, sit down. Have tea, American. And you too, friends of American. Perhaps you will all appear on television in London."

I sat down carefully, squatting toward the back of the small room against a wood pillar. The director nodded to his cameraman, who zoomed in for a close-up.

"*Roshi*, let me ask you one last question—something that confuses us literal-minded liberals back on the British Isles. You speak here constantly of spiritual matters, of enlightenment, of satori, but you are known to be an extremely rich man personally with vast real estate holdings in Kobe and Osaka and a controlling interest in one of Japan's most aggressive new electronics conglomerates—Matsuda. How do you reconcile these two approaches?"

"What is to reconcile?" said the *roshi*, smiling and raising his palms upward. "Does success in spiritual matters necessitate failure in material world? Ask any pope at Vatican. Besides, as we all know, material possessions do not exist. As Doiku told the patriarch Bodhidharma, 'No-thing'—meaning spirit—'is reality.' Thus, if I owned, for example, a Cadillac car, it would not be mine. It only would be passing through me!" He burst out laughing again, jumping up and bouncing around with extraordinary energy. "Ha-ha, very good, no? Mysterious East meets Mysterious West. That is what you should call show. No

. . . Mysterious East meets *Wild* West. Zen cowboy. Bang-bang!" He pointed an imaginary gun at me, then turned to the film crew. "So, it is a wrap, no? Even Zen master must get his sleep. *Ciao, bambini!*"

The film crew gave forth a round of polite thank-yous and began to close up their equipment, most of which was already in its travel cases.

The *roshi* looked at me. "Well, well, American friend. You will stay here, I am sure. You have special interest in Buddhist studies, perhaps intention to proceed to higher spiritual plane."

"I'm interested in being enlightened, if that's what you mean."

"No doubt. No doubt. And that will come swiftly, I will assure you." He clapped his hands and another monk appeared out of nowhere to retrieve the tea materials. "Do not think to leave. As it is written, 'If the buffalo runs, he will fall into the trench.'"

The Brits finished packing their bags and said some final good-byes, the abbot bowing to them with the same copious devotion as Uno. I wondered if he was as skilled in martial matters. Despite the paunch protruding comfortably over his rope belt, I had my suspicions.

"So, my American friend, you have some subject you wish to lay before us?" He sat down again, resuming his lotus position behind the low table and indicating for me, Hodaka, and Uno to follow suit. Behind me, I could hear a motor turn over and the film van start off along the gravel road. Without the camera lights, the illumination had dimmed to a pair of candles and a small bulb lantern in the open corridor leading to another gravel garden.

"It's a matter of blowfish," I said.

"Ah, the blowfish. Interesting animal. Alas, we monks do

not have much experience with it because, as you know, we are vegetarians."

"I'm not talking about an actual blowfish here, *Roshi*. More of an electronic blowfish."

Again behind me, I heard the gate close and a lock being bolted. To my side, I could see Uno's eyes flicker. Hodaka tensed.

"Electronic blowfish. I am not sure I understand what that is. Although I have seen in restaurants such an animal with a bulb inside."

"That's a rather unsophisticated viewpoint for a key investor in the Matsuda Electronics Corporation."

"I only lend them guidance." He bowed his head. "I am just a humble monk—servant of Sakyamuni."

"That's funny. I would imagine you were in control of many facets of the operation. Your representative Mr. Okakura led me to believe you had the ability to see everything, from the corridors of the Imperial Hotel to the most obscure corners of Japanese life."

"Mr. Okakura?" The abbot raised his head and looked at me. "You would have to ask him about that directly." He turned toward the garden where, suddenly, Okakura had silently materialized with about a dozen monks. Even in the half-light, I could see that several of them were carrying weapons—small clubs and short swords—in their waists like modern servants of a theocratic shogun. "You see, American," continued the *roshi*, the relaxed joviality suddenly disappearing from his voice, "you have missed your opportunity. 'Meeting a Zen master on the road,/ Face him neither with words nor silence./ Give him an uppercut/ And you will be called one who understands Zen.' Now it is too late!"

He nodded ever so slightly to Okakura, who shouted some orders to the monks, who drew their weapons and began to advance on us. Considering the odds, I doubted that Uno and

I stood much of a chance, even if he were the aikido champion of a hundred prefectures. And the way Hodaka was shivering, he looked about as useful as a cocker spaniel at a gang rape.

The monks took several more steps forward. I turned to look at the wall behind us. In order to prevent intruders, broken glass had been cemented to the top of the brick in a most unspiritual manner. Down to my right, another trio of monks had materialized, also holding clubs. These monks were wearing hoods that obscured their faces and made them look more medieval than Japanese. I didn't know what any of them wanted to do with us, but my best guess was not croquet. It was one of those moments when I cursed myself for not having finished law school and spent my life reviewing contracts for a middling savings and loan in San Bernadino. I glanced over at Hodaka, who looked within one inch of fainting dead away, when a volley of shots rang out, a consistent volley like an automatic or an AK-47. I dropped to the ground, kissing my ass good-bye, when I noticed the figures of several of Okakura's monks crumpling to the garden floor. They weren't shooting at us. They were shooting at *them*.

I exchanged looks with Hodaka and Uno and the three of us started crawling backward. I saw Okakura go down and the *roshi* himself, struck in the back and stumbling forward in near slow motion like a dying peasant in a Kurosawa movie. His mouth gaping open in astonished pain, he cried out and collapsed onto the gravel in a pool of blood, the perfect concentric circles of his Zen garden scattered into the random disorderliness of a child's sandbox. Then I saw one of the hooded monks begin to smash away at the side of the temple, a weirdly sacrilegious act that seemed somehow centuries old. Simultaneously another of them was turning in our direction. Uno tapped me on the shoulder and we started running for the front gate where, at least, there was no jagged glass to block our way. I dragged the terrified Hodaka along with me as we ran, reaching the door as a line of bullets split the wood right in front of us. Uno, using his shoulder like a battering ram, crashed through it and I ducked low, jumping through after him, another round of shots piercing the air over my head. Hodaka fell, his leg caught in the split wood. I grabbed his arm and pulled him as one of the monks raced toward us, clutching his weapon. He raised it up just as I reached into my jacket, pulled out my pistol, and shot him in the neck. His head snapped back, knocking off his hood and revealing his face.

He was Caucasian.

Not spending a second considering this information, Uno and I took Hodaka by both arms, nearly pulling them out of their sockets, and half yanked, half carried him off into the night, disappearing into the eerie darkness of the neighboring bamboo grove.

12

ACADEMIC APARTMENTS are the same everywhere in the world—walls full of paperback books jammed into gently warping shelves, stacks of old LPs from Vivaldi to the Beatles, art prints (possibly Magritte or some faded pop art), and worn political memorabilia to attest to some measure of commitment to the good of humanity. The apartment in Shinjuku I stood in that night had all those ingredients plus a collection of detective movie posters—copies as far I could tell—from the thirties and forties as well as, in the center of the dining room table, a papier-mâché model of the very Maltese Falcon surrounded by about two dozen bottles of imported booze that must have cost a pretty penny here in the land east of the sun.

The members of the Maltese Falcon Society themselves—a ragtag collection of writers, translators, teachers, critics, and friends of the mystery novel (many of them wearing society T-shirts with a cartoon of Bogie as Sam Spade on the front)— were grouped around me as if I were not a real man myself, but a fictional character, descended in the flesh from the murderous streets of faraway Los Angeles complete with a Lucky Strike dangling from my mouth and a slatternly blonde on my arm. To accommodate them and to anesthetize myself, I consumed as much of their Wild Turkey bourbon as possible, within a few minutes slurring my words and doing a more than passable imitation of a twelfth-rate P.I. on the skids.

Actually what I was feeling was relieved to be alive. We had spent several hours hiding under a teahouse while the hooded monks—there turned out to be six of them—beat their way across the bamboo grove, out the temple complex, and back again searching for us. When I got my second look at them, I confirmed that they were Caucasian all right, but when I heard them muttering to each other, I knew they weren't Caucasians from Cincinnati, or even Philadelphia, but Caucasians from somewhere much closer to the Caucasus themselves—deep in the heart of Mother Russia. They disappeared later to be replaced by the local police who, having heard belated reports of gunfire in the vicinity of the Daitoku-ji Temple, arrived on the scene at about midnight. Once they discovered the carnage at the Daisen-in, they concentrated their efforts in that area and we were able to slip out undetected, returning to Tokyo the next morning, where Hodaka read me the bewildered reportage of the event in the *Mainichi Daily News*.

It seemed that the now-deceased monk—*Roshi* Kokaju— had been under investigation by the Japanese police and by

MITI itself for something euphemistically called "international business fraud" (so much for Okakura having been a MITI man) and that the books of Matsuda Electronics and its small but growing subdivision of Chrysanthemum Computers had been under subpoena. Reading between the lines, Hodaka said it implied that the good Zen master already had one sandal-clad foot in the hoosegow when the hooded men got to him. The question was whether those same hooded men, those "Caucasians," were merely there to execute an unreliable business partner or whether they were after something for their own country. My guess was the latter. And if they had found it—and if it was Blowfish—my further suspicion was that the game was already up.

"Mr. Wine," a man with a wispy beard interrupted my reverie. "What training do you feel is necessary for your occupation?"

"I don't know. I haven't been able to figure that out yet."

"Mr. Wine," Hodaka translated as a thin man in horn-rimmed glasses addressed me. "What is your opinion of detectives who do divorce cases?"

"Same thing as therapists who do divorce cases. It comes with the territory." I took another swig of Wild Turkey. Everybody smiled politely.

"Mr. Wine!" A translator waved his pipe at me, speaking in English. He was a jowly, heavyset man in a traditional kimono, but his hairstyle and sad eyes gave him the all too familiar demeanor of a leftover sixties person still struggling to find himself. "How would you describe the difference between working for a corporation and working for yourself?"

"There's no real difference," I said. "I never work for myself. I always work for a client. Only this time it's a big fat client with stockholders, executives, engineers, and maintenance men."

"And that is the same to you?"

"Hey, you know what Dylan said—'You gotta serve some-body!'" I was being flip and I didn't like what I was saying, but I was half drunk and in a rotten mood anyway, so what was the point? "Look," I said, "you can fuck up a case no matter who you're working for and sometimes you're just over your head. As a two-bit private dick, I was okay because nobody knew or cared what I did anyway, but as security director of Tulip Computers, I'm a washout. The first major league corporate theft that has occurred since I was there has left me completely baffled with not even a rat's ass's worth of the resources to solve it. I'm a total failure."

There was a long, embarrassed silence from the members of the society after Hodaka translated my discourse. Self-revelation was not a highly regarded pastime in Japan. In fact, it was clear they would do almost anything to avoid it. They might have been pressing ahead of us at a rapid clip technolog-ically, but as far as "Me-Generational" personal searches were concerned, they were about three hundred years behind. Maybe they knew something we didn't know.

"Perhaps we can help you," said a woman in the back, clear-ing her voice as she spoke. It was Fumiko. "You know, here in Japan we are very concerned with welfare of group."

"Yeah. So I've heard. Well . . ." I took another swallow of bourbon, this time noticing a slight look of disapproval from the members as I drank, replacing their previous benign amusement at the behavior of a "typical" American gumshoe. "Uh, what we'd need to do is find a Russian. Now, that Russian is a lot more skillful than any of us at what he does—what they call spycraft. And I don't have the slightest idea where he is or indeed whether he is still in Japan." I paused for a moment to let Hodaka translate. "In fact, I only have one pretty ridiculous way of finding him: He likes American jazz, collects American jazz records. . . . Also, I know, there's a bigger audience for jazz here in Japan—and more recording—than there is back in the States now." I stopped again. The society members were listening intently, a classroom filled with good, earnest students. "It's a long shot, but I saw him buy some jazz records in San Francisco and maybe he's been doing the same thing here. I figure this group, considering your interests, must know all the jazz shops in Tokyo, or the important ones anyway, and you could case them for me."

"Ah, case," said Hodaka, brightening up. "'Case the joint'!"

"Right. Only case *all* the joints and find out if a Russian named Viktor Maximov—or for that matter any Russian at all—has been around and where he might be staying or heading. Savvy?"

"Savvy?" Hodaka looked confused.

"Savvy—Tex-Mex for 'understand.' Like *sabe usted* in Spanish."

Hodaka nodded, writing this one down. Then the members of the society started talking with each other in an animated, almost excited fashion. One of them took out a map and started plotting addresses with a Magic Marker, giving each an assignment. Several got up and began to go for their coats. Hodaka turned to me.

"We have decided to adjourn early. Many of the record stores are still open and if you intend to complete your task, we must do it now before this man leaves the country. Besides, it will give us an opportunity to experience detective work firsthand."

And with that the forty-odd group members stood, said good-bye to me, and departed, leaving me standing with Hodaka and Uno in the small apartment of Mr. and Mrs. Isamu Nakashima, a husband-and-wife team of mystery writers who wrote procedural novels about the Osaka police force.

We sat down together around a card table and made small talk for a while, eating sticky rice candies and drinking green tea. Within a half hour the phone rang. Hodaka picked it up, spoke briefly, then turned to me.

"The Shimura Record Center in Roppongi. Yesterday morning Russian buy complete reissue set of Eric Dolphy plus *Thelonious Monk Live at the Five Spot.*"

"Good album," I said. "Let's go."

"Also looking for original Horace Silver *Cookin' at the Continental.* Left phone number."

"Better and better."

Twenty minutes later we were down in Roppongi, heading for Shimura Records. It was a chic area of town with a number of foreigners on the street and a lot of modishly dressed Japanese, girls in loose-fitting gray-flecked jackets, and boys in neo-punk skinny black ties and black leather pants.

The translator with the pipe was standing in front of the store waiting for us when we arrived. He looked incongruous in his tattered kimono against the glitzy background of the local *jeunesse doré.*

"Thanks for the help," I said. "You're brilliant."

"I hope I am not lackey of U.S. corporate imperialism."

"Not a chance. Did you get the number?"

He shook his head. "They were suspicious."

"Who's the clerk?" I asked. The translator pointed. "Wait outside," I said, and signaled for Hodaka to follow me into the store.

I thumbed through some albums, sizing up the clerk for a moment, then walked up to him.

"Horace Silver," I said, affecting a Russian accent that would have barely gotten me a walk-on in a community theater revival of *Anastasia.*

"Ah, Horace Silver, good, good, hard bebop," he replied. I figured that was about the extent of his English. He took an album off the rack and showed it to me.

"I already haf zat one," I said.

"Haf?" The clerk stared at me, totally confused.

I whispered to Hodaka. "Tell him I already have this one. Tell him I have all of them back in Moscow. I'm just missing *Cookin' at the Continental*."

Hodaka stared at me, puzzled for a moment, turned and relayed my message to the clerk, then reported back with the clerk's response. "He says *Cookin' at the Continental* must be very rare album in Russia."

"Ask him why."

Another exchange in Japanese. "He says Russian here the other day asking for same record."

I gasped and made a show of becoming tremendously excited. "Who? Who? Who?" I asked, clutching the clerk by the sleeve. "Was his name Viktor?"

"Viktor! Viktor!" The clerk nodded vehemently, catching the contagion of my enthusiasm.

"Where is he?" I clutched more intensely at the clerk's sleeve but he didn't understand. "Ask him where he is. Tell him he is my cousin!"

Hodaka rolled his eyes briefly, then translated for the clerk. "Cousin! Cousin!" I repeated.

"*Hai, hai* . . . cousin," said the clerk, now beginning to recognize the word. But he seemed reluctant to do anything about it.

Ignoring this, I did a jump for joy, spinning in midair and shouting "My cousin! My cousin!" Then I clenched my fists, crying out ecstatically, squatted on the floor, and started dancing the *kazatski*, hands on hips, kicking my legs full force while singing some fantasy version of "Midnight in Moscow" at the top of my lungs, making up the words in mock Russian à la Peter Ustinov. By now everyone in the store was staring at me in shock and amazement. I only increased my tempo, bending over on my hands and going into a dizzying spin I somehow dimly remembered from a college film society screening of

Alexander Nevsky. The reserved Japanese were mortified—this was definitely not their style—especially the clerk, who, now red-faced and feeling completely responsible for this unseemly public display, breathlessly rushed around his counter, almost knocking over a bin of Seiko Matsuda records, to retrieve a slip of paper taped to the side of the cash register.

Thirty seconds later I was emerging from the store clutching Maximov's phone number and smiling in amusement at Hodaka, who was muttering under his breath about how my technique was not sufficiently "hard-boiled" to fit his literary image of proper detective behavior. Perhaps he would have preferred me to beat the clerk to a bloody pulp. Personally, I had already had enough violence here in pacifist Japan to last me for the next thirty years.

I thanked the sad-eyed translator once again and said good-bye to him, heading for the Roppongi subway station with Hodaka and Uno before we even checked out Maximov's number. The image of Yasuko/Laura had come into my mind and I kept wondering about her anger, where it all came from. I finally stopped at a red phone right at the entrance to the station and was about to pass the number over to Hodaka when I realized that I recognized it already, but I double-checked it with the matchbook in my pocket just to make sure. I was right. It was the switchboard of the Imperial Hotel.

Standing at the hotel's north entrance, by a five-story annex of shops that looked as if they catered to visiting oil sheiks, I briefly contemplated my situation. I was clearly dealing with a man who was my definite superior in practically all aspects of a trade I had fallen into quite accidentally.

There was little doubt that he had tracked my every move, even to the point of registering at the same hotel I had chosen by whim from an airplane guidebook. And now Blowfish, whatever it was, was in his possession, probably already in the hands of some institute in the Novosibirsk, where they were struggling to decode its unfathomable technical intricacies.

And yet there was something that did not parse in all this. In some peculiar way it had all been too easy for me—the death of Rigrod, the tracking of Laura, the black curtain man, artificial intelligence, Blowfish, Cassiopeia. Yes, Cassiopeia, that was the strange one. Little blips across my home computer screen that had led me here to Tokyo in guided clues seemingly cryptic but not quite cryptic enough, certainly not opaque. A chill wind blew up off Hibiya Park and suddenly I began to feel even more out of my depth. I glanced over at my allies—sweet Hodaka and loyal Uno—and knew they would be useless to me from here on in. No longer was it a question of translation or of a few swift martial arts kicks. From here on in, the war would be won with the mind and I wondered, in this world of synchronicity and proliferating electronic impulses, if I was up to it, indeed if any man, acting by himself, would ever be up to it again.

Against their better wishes and urgent protestations, I sent Hodaka and Uno home. Then I walked into the huge lobby of the hotel and picked up a house phone, staring across at the immense cocktail lounge where yellow and white men in expensive suits sat opposite each other exchanging pleasantries and making mega-deals.

"Viktor Maximov's room, please."

The operator connected me. Seconds later a Russian voice answered. "Maximov."

"Mr. Maximov, this is Moses Wine. I'm in the lobby at the moment and I'd like to come up and speak to you. I think we have some important matters to discuss."

There was a moment of hesitation, then: "1908." I knew the room well. It was four doors down from mine.

"See you in a couple of minutes," I said, but then I realized the line was already dead.

Feeling slightly dizzy and weightless, I began the long walk across the lobby, down a long corridor, and up a flight of stairs to the tower elevator. Along the way, uniformed girls with white gloves bowed to me with excessive politeness as if my very presence in the hotel were an honor to the establishment of incomprehensible scope. I ignored them, trying to concentrate my mind. Cassiopeia, I kept thinking, Cassiopeia high in the firmament, who are you?

The elevator opened out onto the nineteenth floor and I turned a corner that ended in a floor-to-ceiling window over half of Tokyo, a wall of blazing neon. Room 1908 was four doors down and I approached carefully, not expecting any violence here in the Imperial Hotel, but cautious nevertheless. Maximov obviously had a small army at his command.

I knocked on the door and it was opened by a strapping blond-haired youth who looked like something out of the changing of the guard at Lenin's Tomb. He looked back at Maximov, who was seated in a green Empire-style chair facing the other way and staring out at the Japanese light show beneath him. I figured they didn't have anything like that in Moscow. I knew they didn't have anything like that in San Francisco either.

"Come in, Mr. Wine," he said, simultaneously turning in his chair and nodding to the youth, who retreated through a door. It was then that I realized we were in a suite. The GRU could treat its people well. "A drink." He indicated a well-stocked bar. "I understand you like bourbon . . . as well as what are known in your country as 'controlled substances.' "

I smiled. "You probably know more about me than my mother, Maximov."

"As far as the details of one's life are concerned, one's mother is the least likely source after the age of eleven."

"True," I said, studying Maximov more closely. He was more East Russian than I had remembered, with thick, high cheekbones and a heavy-lidded aspect, as if he were peering out at you through the slats of a rifle sight with only the slightest portion of his cornea showing, a human one-way mirror. I turned to peruse the bar again. As well as a plentiful collection of hard liquor, there was a wide selection of hors d'oeuvres—a cheese dip, caviar, oysters, and sashimi. "I think I'll try some of your home brew," I said, selecting a bottle of Stolichnaya and pouring a generous amount over ice. "I like the hors d'oeuvres too. Of course, I wouldn't trust the sashimi. You never know with raw fish."

"Indeed. Although here in Japan the incidence of salmonella and similar diseases is quite low. For a capitalist country, they are extremely advanced in matters of public health."

"You're right about that. I suppose nothing could really happen to you . . . as long as you stay away from blowfish."

"Yes, blowfish is another matter entirely."

I picked up my glass and toasted him casually, letting my eyes drift around the room. As I expected, everything seemed to be hotel issue, with the exception of about a dozen jazz records stacked up on the television set. I walked over and started to thumb through the stack.

"You like Clifford Brown and Max Roach?" I asked, seeing one of my favorites.

"Of course, a dead trumpet prodigy with the finest drummer who ever lived. But let us not waste time, Mr. Wine. Surely you did not come here to discuss jazz. And do not think because I know who you are, because I know about your background in the anti-war movement, civil rights, and so forth, that I will be sympathetic to you. Those are the very Americans I most distrust. In my country they would be dissidents. Nixon and Reagan would be in the Politburo."

I looked him straight in the eye. "Well . . . it's about Blowfish."

"Of course it is."

"I imagine it's giving you some trouble."

"Really? How so?"

"I don't think it's what you expected it to be."

"And what did I expect?"

"I don't know. You're a trained engineer, I'm not."

"Then how would you know?"

"It's just a hunch."

"A hunch?" He laughed under his breath. "Now I must listen to hunches from computer illiterates?"

"In fact, I'd go so far as to say you don't have the slightest idea what it is. It's garbage as far as you're concerned."

Maximov looked bored—or pretended to. "Finish your vodka, Mr. Wine, and leave. I have a late flight and I still have some packing to do."

"Then I make no sense to you?"

The Russian shrugged, then stood and walked over to his closet. He opened it to reveal a half dozen well-tailored suits. He didn't travel light, this one.

"I guess your laboratories were able to discern its contents in a short time then."

"You can store a lot of information on a 512-kilobyte disk, Mr. Wine."

"Especially if it's bogus."

He turned and looked at me impatiently.

"What if I told you that disk was a total phony? That it was made up to send me here and have you chase after me while the real ace was being palmed elsewhere?"

He didn't say anything.

"How'd you find out about Blowfish in the first place? From telephone conversations monitored from the roof of your San Francisco consulate? Or from that little GRU strip artist masquerading as Miss Polish Solidarity in Silicon Valley? Come on, Maximov, there's no reason to be coy about this. You don't want to go back to the Kremlin looking like a monkey any more than I want to go back empty-handed to—"

"Your corporation?"

"Whatever. I can prove to you for sure that the disk is a fake—that is, if you still have a copy of it."

"No one can do that, Mr. Wine."

"Not even Yasuko Tadao?"

"And I suppose you know where she is."

"As of yesterday."

Now Maximov was studying me through those slatted heavy-lidded eyes of his. After a moment he crouched down in the closet, unlocked an attaché case, and removed a Sony-style three-and-one-half-inch single-sided disk which he tucked into his inside jacket pocket next to his shoulder holster. Then he stood and faced me. "All right, Mr. Wine. Take me to Yasuko Tadao."

"Great, Maximov. But I'd just like to do one thing first."

"What's that?"

I quickly cocked my arm and let him have a hard right cross straight to the jaw. He staggered backward, grasping the bar top.

"Now we're even," I said.

13

HE MAY HAVE BEEN trying to hide it, but something resembling a good old-fashioned capitalist smirk curled around Maximov's lips as we drove into the lot of the Magnificent Magnificent Love Hotel. We were in another Nissan President with Lenin's guard at the wheel next to another bodyguard known affectionately as Mitya. Maximov and I were in the back, staring through curtained windows like a pair of *apparatchiks* on the way to their country dacha. We parked a few yards from the gangplank and I turned to Maximov before getting out.

"I hope you don't mind, but I'd like to see her for a few minutes myself before you come in. I wouldn't worry about it, though. After all"—I tapped his jacket pocket—"you've got the disk."

"Mr. Wine, for the moment, this is your show."

"Thank you, Mr. Maximov." I reached for the door. "Oh, one other thing. Your information on Yasuko Tadao—what does it tell you about her background?"

"Born in Yokohama, June fourth, 1961. Educated—"

"No, no, her parents. Where were *they* born?"

"Nagasaki."

"That's what I figured. It had to be one of the two. And when did they die? In the early sixties, I should imagine."

"Correct."

"Thanks. Let's go."

We got out of the car and started up the gangplank, looking for all the world like a quartet of *gaijin* out for a night on the town. The glass door parted for us and we walked into the lobby, Aunt Akiko looking up in startled panic when she saw me. I looked from her disfigured face to the corridor, which was now sealed off with a heavy steel door.

"Yasuko," I said.

The old woman shook her head vigorously, the most vehement act of determined negation I had ever seen from a Japanese.

"Do any of your people speak the language?" I asked Maximov.

He nodded toward the heroic blond.

"Have him tell her it's very important I see Yasuko, that she won't come to any harm."

Maximov looked at me briefly, then complied, and in about a minute the information came back to me in double translation.

"She says Yasuko is sick. She thinks she is dying. She doesn't want to see anyone."

"Yasuko's probably been worried about that for years. Tell her if she doesn't let me see her we'll blow the place up. Show a little firepower."

"I don't need your instructions," Maximov snapped back at me. But he went ahead and said a few words to his man, who relayed them to Aunt Akiko. Her expression went from panic to dread, her lips beginning to quiver and her left hand shaking with a palsy I hadn't noticed before. She reached under the counter and pressed a button that unlatched the steel door.

"Make yourselves comfortable, guys." I nodded to the photographic display of the hotel rooms and headed through the door down the corridor to the suite at the end.

The door was ajar when I got there, Yasuko lurking in the entryway looking pale and wan in a blue and white print bathrobe. Her hair was bedraggled and spread across her shoulders with the faint hint of a Medusa-like madness. Her eyes were hollowed out, dark globes of smudged makeup. She looked like someone who had taken a week's worth of barbiturates but still hadn't been able to get to sleep. In a way, you could have predicted this. Her life had come crashing down around her in the past few days, ten or fifteen years of preplanned vengeance ending in the lonely oblivion of betrayal.

"I don't know how to say this but . . . in a small way . . . I can guess how you feel. I went to Germany once and I couldn't stand it, left in less than twenty-four hours, even though I only lost some distant relatives I never knew. But for you, all that time in America . . ."

She half nodded as I walked into the room. One of the bedroom blankets was balled in a lump on the living room floor as if she had curled up with it, her thumb in her mouth, in a fetal pose of regression.

"Did they both die before you knew them?"

For a moment she didn't answer, just stood there staring past me, her jaw slightly slack, her lower lip pursing like an animal gasping for air. "No. I . . . remember my father . . . from when I was two or three. He was the lucky one. He was inside when . . ."

Her voice trailed off. "It went off," I said, hesitating before continuing to confirm my suspicions. "So they both died of it then . . . the leukemia . . . shortly after you were born . . . fifteen years after the fact."

"Goddamn you! I don't have to talk to you about this. You Americans dropped that bomb on Nagasaki! The war was already over!" She turned on me suddenly with a hatred that seemed bottomless. It felt pointless, even self-serving, to remind her that I was scarcely fourteen months old when the deed was done. "Don't you understand?" she continued. "It's inherited. I have it too. I know it. I've always had it. It's in my blood! I'll never get it out!" She clutched her arms as if trying to wrench the cancer cells from her veins and then collapsed on the couch, sobbing, her head in her hands.

I sat down beside her, waiting for the tears to subside. I knew enough about leukemia to know the odds were she was lying to herself, but in her present state I didn't think she wanted to hear that, especially from me. After a minute the crying stopped and she started to breathe in long, slow breaths like someone taking air from an oxygen tank. At length she spoke again: "When I was around twelve, someone came to visit me in school. I was doing very well in class—in math and science—and they asked me if I would perform a special mission for Japan. It made me feel very important . . . like I was doing something for my parents. Aunt Akiko said I should go. I never saw that man again. I never saw any of them. In fact, for years I just received instructions—do this, do that, never anything specific until—"

"Until they asked you to get Blowfish."

She nodded.

"Did it ever occur to you that you might not really be working for Japan, that it might just have been private citizens exploiting you for their own gain?"

"I believed Aunt Akiko!" She turned on me angrily again, but then quickly looked away.

And whom did Aunt Akiko believe, I wondered. Some monk talking about the lost glory of Imperial Japan? Some emissary of an embryonic trading company that later became Matsuda Electronics? It didn't matter. It only had to start and then Yasuko/Laura was left twisting in the wind of Gardena, Encino, and Pasadena. "It must feel doubly weird for you," I said, "being back here. You may hate us, but to do what you did, you were forced to become an American." She didn't reply. "Look," I said, trying to sound casual, "I don't know if this is going to interest you anymore, but Blowfish is here."

She stared up at me, startled, her eyes bulging again from their dark sockets.

"I retrieved it from a roundabout source. I presume you've seen it—read the disk, I mean."

She shook her head. "It could only be read by a Bulb computer."

It could only be read by a Bulb computer? Now I was troubled. Maybe this was the real Blowfish and I would be exposing its contents to a Russian agent. "Why didn't you boot it up?" I asked.

"All the prototypes were locked up when I found it—or occupied."

"And you didn't want to wait?"

She looked at me almost angrily. "Moses, I thought my assignment was to bring Blowfish back to Mita Kokusai as soon as possible. For the glory of Japan. How was I to know—"

"You'd been duped from the start and the black-shirted man and his cohorts were waiting at the border to steal it."

She nodded wearily. "Anyway, I didn't think any of this mattered at the time. I didn't have to boot up Blowfish back in Silicon Valley."

"Why not?"

"I had a Bulb prototype right here. I sneaked it out three months earlier under the pretense that it was being sent to a software manufacturer in England."

"What do you mean, here?"

"Here." She pointed straight down. "In the basement."

There was a knock on the door. Oh, shit, I thought—Maximov. Before I could react, he had pushed his way through the door followed by his minions.

"Viktor Maximov—Yasuko Tadao. Ms. Tadao has volunteered to demonstrate Blowfish for us. Shall we?"

I pointed through the door. Yasuko stared at me, puzzled, but I suspected her scientific curiosity would get the better of her, and I was right. In a minute she got up and began to lead us out, down the corridor to a spiral staircase leading to the basement of the stationary boat. Akiko watched us as we went, the atomic lesions on her face turned scarlet under the fluorescent light.

We came to a basement room and Yasuko opened a heavy steel door. A number of late-model American microcomputers were lined up on tables, including products of GTI, Apple, and others. The Bulb was on a table of its own in the corner, looking brand-new, almost cheerful, in its pleasantly designed oval enclosure, which, I knew, had been at Witherspoon's insistence against the wishes of the Wiz, who thought of it as cosmetic hype.

Maximov handed Yasuko the disk, and she sat down on a metal folding chair facing the computer, the rest of us grouping behind her. I suddenly began to experience an emotion I had never felt before, an intense feeling of patriotism coupled with an extreme guilt that I was about to give away state secrets to an enemy of my country. But how could that be? Tulip was a personal computer company. What they did was of interest primarily to their competitors. And from what I knew, the Russians were not about to go into the consumer microcomputer business. They had enough trouble providing their citizenry with refrigerators. And besides, it was this or nothing. Bulb computers would soon be on sale to everybody. Were I not here, sooner or later the Russians would have cracked the code, if there was any, and had Blowfish all to themselves.

So I held my breath as Yasuko turned on the computer, inserted the disk into the drive, and booted up. There was a brief whir and then, in less than a second, the Tulip logo appeared on the screen, unfurling from a bulb to a full flower in a brilliant display of high-resolution graphics many times finer than the NBC peacock. This held for a couple of seconds, following a beep, and then a message faded up on the screen:

```
This is a restricted program. Enter your
password please.
```

Yasuko immediately typed in Black Widow 375XCT. That would have taken the Russians a little time, I thought. After some further whirring, another message appeared:

```
Welcome      to      Blowfish_an      artificial
intelligence game written in the PROLOG
programming language. The object of this
game   is   to   achieve   satori,   or
enlightenment. . . . Would you like to
try? Y/N
```

Yasuko pressed Y. The response came back instantly:

```
Wrong. You cannot achieve enlightenment
by trying. Trying is lying. Would you
like to try again? Y/N
```

This time she pressed N. The response came back even faster:

```
Better. You understand that trying is an
illusion. Now let us consider the story
of the two monks who approached the
river . . .
```

"It's a fucking computer game!" said Maximov, now resorting to the most colloquial of English.

"That's right," I said. "As I told you, we've all been on a wild-goose chase . . . some of us—unfortunately—for longer than others." I looked at Yasuko but she had her eyes fixed on the screen with an expression of utter desolation. I wanted to reach out and touch her, but something inside me said she would only respond by cringeing and withdrawing further into herself. The unfortunate truth of the matter was, given her sad history, she had become nothing but a human shell, a living dead person—and would probably be that way for the rest of her natural life. There was little I or anybody else could do to change it.

"Look," I said, "why don't we simplify matters?" I flicked off the machine and rebooted the system disk, immediately running the copy program and picking up a couple of blank diskettes from the side of the machine. "We'll make one of these for each of us." The others stood there as I went right ahead, too stunned to object or do anything about it. The fast-working Bulb spit out the copies in a matter of seconds. "Here," I said, handing one to Yasuko, returning the original to Maximov, and keeping one for myself. "Now we're all even.

We can, uh, have a contest. See who achieves peace of mind first. But you guys gotta give me a head start. I've been in a mid-life crisis!"

And with that I walked out of the room.

14

I DIDN'T BELIEVE IT when I heard Sara had taken up with the Wiz. I had, after all, been out of the country for less than a week and the Wiz, I had thought, was at least somewhat involved with the ungainly Stanford biogeneticist. Moreover, I didn't have the faintest idea they even knew each other.

But seeing was believing—and as I stood with my younger son, Simon, among the excited crowd of stockholders and media gathered in the Padre Serra room of the San Jose Hyatt for the long-awaited unveiling of the Bulb computer, there he was on the podium, smiling and waving to admirers with a relaxation I had never seen before while holding hands with my putative girl friend. No wonder she had sounded so evasive when I had phoned her the previous evening from the international baggage claim at LAX.

Even Simon was confused. He had met her once before, during a period when Sara and I were getting along better, and had assumed we were still together. In fact, he had asked about her when I picked him up in L.A.—fresh with his Maui suntan—at his mother's new Mulholland Drive Mediterranean Estate to take him up north for a long weekend. Not that it was of great concern to him. By now, like most California kids, he had developed a built-in defense mechanism against the comings and goings, couplings and uncouplings, of his parents' generation. It was a question of survival, yet another turn in the evolution of our species.

Still it baffled him and it baffled me that Sara and the Wiz were so lovey-dovey on the podium at the Bulb unveiling. The event itself had grown out of all proportion, the Wiz's celebrity coupled with the supposed cutthroat competition with GTI for the next-generation microcomputer market making good copy for the various hacks and flacks of the national press and the already overstuffed computer media. This was the Gunfight at the OK Corral—the last stand of the free and independent entrepreneur against the man-eating multinational. Free enterprise was on trial and America loved it. They were lined up from Bakersfield to North Beach just to see—or at least as far out the door as the Hyatt parking lot where, like at a rock concert, a large video screen had been erected for closed-circuit projection to accommodate the overflow crowd.

On the rostrum, behind Wiz, were his attendant spirits, the Knights of his Round Table, those legions of software and hardware developers who had come from as near as Marin County and as far as Boston to pledge their support to his mighty endeavor. Lined up on ergonomically designed office chairs, dressed in denims and safari jackets, they constituted a new business elite, honed on the technological cutting edge and tempered by the activism of the late sixties and early seventies, to create a new center of glamour to replace Hollywood and Washington. They were arrogant; they were strong; they were young; they were brilliant. And they all wanted to be rich, if they weren't already.

So, for that matter, did I. For beneath the golden glow of idealism hanging heavily over the occasion was the eager lust of greed. And not one of us attending the event could say he was immune to it, not even Simon, who, by his own admission, "didn't like computers" but was a devotee, at that moment, of break dancing, almost an equal fad for those more physically inclined. Even he, at age twelve, wanted to know what the success or failure of the Bulb would "do to the stock."

"For this computer," said the Wiz, speaking through a cordless mike with a nearly stutter-free authority, "we have built the fastest assembly line in America, one machine every t-twenty-three seconds. When we first made the Tulip Ii, back in the garage in 1976, we were producing barely fifty computers a month. Now, in 1984, we plan to produce the Bulb at the rate of one million a year. By the end of the summer, every one of these p-people"—he pointed to the group behind him—"will be manufacturing software or hardware add-ons for this machine. We encourage the greatest creative minds of our time to work on it, make it their tool, their servant, to build a t-true computer democracy for those who understand the technology and for those who d-do not!"

There was a burst of applause. A band broke into an up-tempo chorus of Michael Jackson's "Beat It," and balloons started falling from a rigging carrying giveaway T-shirts with the Tulip logo silkscreened on the back. It was a curious reminder of my recent farewell to Japan when Hodaka and several members of the Maltese Falcon Society drove me to the airport and gravely presented me with a souvenir T-shirt of their society to commemorate my visit as an "honored guest." I was peculiarly touched.

"Well, well, super sleuth, back from the Orient?" I looked over to see Witherspoon standing beside me. "Enjoying the show?"

"Sure. Everybody loves a parade. How come you're not up on the podium?"

"Oh, this is Wiz's day. I wouldn't want to steal it from him. I'm just a behind-the-scenes manager. Any luck with your investigation?"

"Not a bit. Round-trip ticket to nowhere."

"That's strange." He looked at me with an expression that showed no disappointment.

"Not half as strange as coming back here to find the Black Widow offices shut down . . . cleaned out and swept clean as if nobody had ever been there."

"Well. . . ." He shrugged.

"Blowfish turned out to be a computer game."

"Really?"

"Uh-huh. I've been trying to reach the Wiz, but he's been incommunicado since I got back."

"He's been busy, obviously." Witherspoon gestured toward the stage. "Put it in a memo."

"A memo! Look, some people have been murdered. Over in Japan, half a monastery's worth of monks had their guts blown out by Russian assault weapons. If this really is a game, there's a hell of a penalty for the winners and losers. I need a Bulb computer. Right now. For my personal use!"

"I don't know if that's possible. They're in such short supply until the assembly line's going full steam. And we've promised the first batch to our suppliers."

"Are you bullshitting my father?" said Simon, who had been listening to our conversation.

"Excuse me?" said Witherspoon. I grinned as he stared down at Simon with the look of someone with four generations of WASP training about what children should be seen instead of.

"My dad's a detective and people lie to him a lot. You know, like on TV."

Witherspoon blanched. Good boy, I thought, you're worth your weight in break dancers. "This is my son Simon. Simon, this is Mr. Witherspoon."

"Yes, I see," said Witherspoon, nodding haughtily. "Nice to see you again, Wine . . . and, uh, Simon." He started off.

"Wait a minute, Mal. How about that computer?"

"Have your girl call my secretary."

"You mean your area associate."

"Yes, of course, my *area associate*."

He walked off with the pained expression of an emergency hemorrhoid victim.

"Think he's guilty, Dad?" asked Simon.

"Of something."

I started to turn back to the stage—where the Wiz was introducing some visiting celebrities who had come to bless the occasion, including Stewart "Whole Earth" Brand and Ex-Gov Jerry Brown—when I noticed another familiar face out of the corner of my eye. It was Alf Richardson, Rigrod's old roommate. For a split second our eyes locked, then he looked away and started sidestepping to his right, first slowly, glancing back to see if I was watching, then more quickly, slithering through the crowd like a snake.

"Is he guilty too?"

"Of something."

Simon thought for a second. "Everybody's guilty of something, huh?"

"You could say that."

"What about that guy?" he asked, nodding to my left, where I saw my old friend Herb Shear, standing with a walkie-talkie, observing the proceedings. "He's been watching you too."

"He's a cop."

Simon frowned. "They could be guilty too, couldn't they?"

I didn't bother answering him. I was too busy watching Sara turn and give Wiz an adoring kiss straight on the lips right in front of two thousand people.

It was hard to get out of my head as I sat in front of a Bulb computer in my house that night, trying to make sense of the operating system. It was supposed to be the most user-friendly machine ever produced, but this particular user's powers of concentration had been reduced to powdered Kool-Aid. I felt like I was back in high school trigonometry, wrestling with sine, cosine, and tangent and drawing the solemn conclusion that mine was not to be a life of science.

Besides, I had no right to be so addled. My relationship with Sara was never meant to be "exclusive." Indeed, *I* had not behaved that way from the first. Yet here I was, blindly moving the computer mouse back and forth like a talisman on a Ouija board while Simon played with Toto as if it were the family dog. (To keep him entertained while I worked, I had programmed the robot to answer to his voice.)

"Fetch, Toto, fetch," Simon would say, tossing a tennis ball across the living room.

The little machine would waddle across the room, pick up the ball, and practically crush it with his pincer before returning it to a circular ashtray in front of Simon.

I finally got the computer to boot up when I heard Simon say "Toto, find a girl friend. Find a girl friend, Toto."

"Toto does not understand 'girl friend.' "

"Who does?" I muttered, once more staring at the words: This is a restricted program. Enter your password please. I quickly typed in Yasuko's code, Black Widow 375XCT, which I had burned indelibly on my memory. In a moment I was back on the path to enlightenment, answering such inscrutable questions as What is mu? and Has a dog Buddha-nature? To the latter I answered No, but my robot has. The computer replied: Do not be whimsical. This is the most serious question of all. If you say yes or no, you lose your own Buddha-nature.

Wonderful, I thought. Here I was playing ask-me-another with a 32-bit integrated circuit when a killer(s) was running around loose. But I was no closer to who it was than when Witherspoon had first informed me of Rigrod's death over a week ago. One thing, though, seemed likely to me, and had for a long time—neither Maximov nor one of his minions had murdered Danny Rigrod. They were far too professional to do away with a well-known American computer scientist in that manner, especially one who was known to have been palling around with a "representative" of the Polish Solidarity Movement in a Silicon Valley bar. Besides, if they had, it made even less sense that they would be nosing around his roommate's house the next evening, checking out the scene. More likely, they were as stunned as everybody else.

And what of the so-called Blowfish? Now that I had retrieved it for the Wiz, I couldn't even get him on the phone. Wasn't that a paradigm of corporate life? Kill the messenger who brings the bad news. It wasn't my fault it turned out to be a second-rate computer game and not some glorious computer add-on with miraculous capabilities. Not that I really believed that. I was positive the disk was not Blowfish at all, but a decoy, a trap set by some sonofabitch willing to send me halfway around the world to get my ass in a sling . . . as well as unleash a series of forces drawn taut on the three great powers of the world—Russia, the U.S.A., and Japan. Who knew? Maybe it was a two-tiered game, two-tiered like Blowfish, being played out on one level by large corporate entities and nation-states and on another by human beings struggling desperately for survival in this sad vale of tears.

What I suspected was that the author of the game, the one who had sprung this little trap, was the one who either offed Rigrod or had a good idea who did. I thought for a moment and jotted down the names that came to mind—Alf Richardson, Eddie Capshaw, and, reluctantly, the Wiz. They were the only ones I could think of with enough knowledge of Rigrod's activities, coupled with the requisite skill to write this disk and send Yasuko on her merry way. Of course, there had to be others. This was a valley filled with wild-card hackers willing to knock out a quick-and-dirty source code for a few tanks of gas and the chance for a little publicity. But I doubted, as hard as I would look, that I would find the signature of the programmer on this one, even though pride of authorship had become a serious bone of contention of late in the boom-or-bust software world.

But still, there might have been a signature of another sort in this game, so I pushed on, negotiating the thicket of booby-trapped homilies, when a peculiarly familiar set of phrases appeared on my screen. `Meeting a Zen master on the road, face him neither with words nor silence. Give him an uppercut and you will be called one who understands Zen.` I remembered immediately that those were the words of Kokaju, the now-deceased abbot of Daisen-in. How strange to see them repeated here in the midst of this computer program, though I assumed they were a famous Buddhist parable of some sort, the meaning of which, as far as I could understand it, was that the road to enlightenment was not through another, but through oneself. I didn't know how that helped me at the moment, unless I had stolen Blowfish myself without knowing it. And besides, the only person I had given an uppercut in the last five years was Maximov—and as far as I could tell, he was hardly a Zen master.

`All right, smart guy,` I typed into the computer. `Who killed Danny Rigrod?`

`Every being is inherently without a flaw` came the reply.

`Well, who do you think killed him?`

`Thought is the sickness of the human mind.`

How informative, I thought. Obviously this game was not getting me very far. It was time to return to conventional methods.

My next move was to go see Alf Richardson, but I didn't know what to do about Simon. I would have taken him with me, but the last time I had gone to visit Rigrod's ex-roommate, the results had hardly been benign. And considering what could be lurking in the night, I didn't feel comfortable leaving a twelve-year-old by himself under the protection of a robot either, especially the fourth one off the assembly line. So I bit the bullet and called Sara.

"I'm sorry, Moses," she said. "I'd like to help you, but I have a previous engagement."

"Oh, yeah, with that poor little multimillionaire prodigy."

"Don't get smart, Moses. You didn't know how to commit and you lost out. Besides, Wiz may be a multimillionaire, but he's got his problems too. Everybody's pain is finite."

"Thank you, Joyce Brothers," I said, and hung up, typing the words Fuck Sara into the machine before flicking it off. The computer replied: Lovely vocabulary you have. Who was your mother? I typed back: Fuck Zen. The computer replied: You are drawing closer to enlightenment. I answered: Fuck enlightenment. Fuck computers. Fuck it all. Fuck Blowfish! There was a pause as the computer shuffled through its artificial intelligence files, trying to make sense of my frustrated screed. Finally the words System error on 35 appeared on the screen, followed by the sentence Blowfish is sea moss. Sea moss, I thought? Jesus! And flicked off the bloody thing!

I drove over to Richardson's in the BMW with Simon in the front seat with me and Toto in the back, swiveling his head around and blinking his eyes like the Tin Woodsman on a holiday. It was pitch dark when we got there. The garage was closed and the windows shuttered. An eerie northeasterly wind blew up from across the valley, rustling the leaves of the live oaks. We got out of the car and started down the driveway for the front door. A crack of light was visible, coming from the bedroom area, but not as bright as the type usually used to deter robbers. I clutched Simon's hand, holding him close to me, with Toto waddling right behind us, his joints squeaking like a rusty gate. It sounded like he needed a lube job.

We got to the front door and I knocked several times with no response. I cocked my ear. From inside, I could hear the sound of Judy Garland singing "But Not for Me" repeating on a broken record. I listened for a moment, then I circled around to the garage and pulled it open. The Mercedes turbo-diesel, the Jeep, and the silver Porsche were still sitting in their places, a thin patina of dust gathered on the Mercedes' graphite hood. I hurried back to Simon, feeling apprehensive and protective. I took his hand again and hurried back to the front door, where Toto was waiting, his lights blinking like a Christmas tree ornament.

"Bash it, Toto!" I said.

"Toto does not understand 'Bash it.' "

"Break the door down!"

A grinding whir of gears came from the area that would have been his stomach and he moved his pincer arm directly backward, turning it about like a corkscrew until it sprang forward with an astonishing force that split the heavy pine like balsa, creating a hole the size of a medicine ball and twisting the wrought-iron hinges right out of their jambs. The door went crashing to the floor with a resounding shot that echoed across the canyon; a covey of crows screeched out of the trees like ominous shadows across the Milky Way.

"Toto watch Simon," I said, and proceeded into the house on my own.

It appeared to be empty and I was right that the one small light came from the bedroom. I walked down toward it, along a dark hall, Judy Garland's voice repeating, ad infinitum, from the stereo. The bedroom too was nearly dark. There were a couple of half-filled suitcases opened on the mattress, piles of clothes stacked at random, as if someone were packing in a hurry. The sole light I had seen was not a bulb but the glow of yet another computer CRT sitting on an endtable beside an empty vial of cocaine, the words HOW COULD HE LOVE HER? writ large in amber across the screen. An eight-by-ten photograph was visible in its reflection, half crumpled and torn seemingly in anger on the tabletop in front of it. I unfolded it and stared at the shiny figures. It was a color snap of Rigrod and Richardson in a woodsy hot tub, their smiling bodies locked in a naked embrace.

I put it down and started for the other rooms when I heard a door slam, followed immediately by the supercharged *varoom* of what could only be the Porsche. Making a quick about-face, I ran for the front door, emerging just as the sports car was shooting out of the driveway.

"Go to the car!" I shouted to Simon. "Into the BMW, Toto!"

"Toto does not understand 'Into the BMW.' "

"Oh, fuck. Get in the car."

The robot waddled over to the front and started to open the hood.

"Not that, you metal-brained bag of silicon! Get *into* the car!"

The machine finally climbed into the back seat. "Buckle up!" I said to Simon, who was already ensconced beside me as I watched the Porsche turn right onto the winding hilltop road. "You too, tin man!" I added, revving the motor and checking the rearview mirror where, improbably enough, the robot was visible buckling *his* seat belt.

I pulled out the turbo-charger and hit the gas, wheeling out of the driveway in a cloud of dirt after the other car. I was nervous about Simon, but secretly pleased finally to have a chance to use the souped-up BMW Wiz had given me. And unlike Japan, the road was clear, a long, twisting test run for my car and the Porsche.

I swung out of the driveway in second, the MacPherson struts leaning rightward and springing back with amazing control. The other car was not visible, but I slid into third immediately, hitting the straightaway with an acceleration I had never felt before, like a test pilot in a centrifuge. Within five seconds the speedometer was reading seventy-five and climbing. I jumped it from third to fifth, catching a glimpse of the speeding Porsche up ahead of me. I was gaining on it at a fantastic clip. The road started to weave in tight S's, banking sharply against the side of the mountain. I held tight, swaying with the turns, drawing ever closer to the sports car.

Then, suddenly, the Porsche slowed as if it had slipped out of gear. I drew up right behind, my headlights blasting into its rear, when it turned abruptly through a heavily wooded area and picked up steam. I lost sight of it briefly, then saw it again blasting full throttle straight ahead of me with the door half open. I barreled after it, right into a hard left turn, but it kept going straight, as if its steering column had locked, crossed the center divider, and flew directly off the edge of the road into a deep ravine, rolling over several times. I screeched to a halt just as the Porsche crashed into a large granite outcropping at the bottom of the ravine, bursting into flames and sending shards of metallic shrapnel flying twenty yards in every direction.

I told Simon to wait, got out of the car, and descended the ravine to the burning vehicle. It took me a couple of minutes to negotiate the steep terrain. When I arrived, the Porsche was already a smoldering wreck with a few dying flames licking at the side of what remained of the chassis. The inert body of Alf Richardson was lying on its back about thirty feet ahead, his skull cracked against a rock as if he had been pitched from the car on impact and thrown forward or had flown out while it was rolling down the ravine. The whole scene had a strange still-life quality to it—the car, the body, the granite outcropping—but it didn't stop me from feeling sick. I clutched the branch of a tree and took a deep breath to stop myself from throwing up.

Thirty minutes later I was down at San Jose Airport, putting

Simon on the last plane back to L.A. This was a world of violence, and I'd be a horse's ass if I was going to expose a twelve-year-old to more of it.

15

"I TOLD YOU to stay out of this." Herb Shear looked exhausted and fed up as I followed him down the corridor to his office at one o'clock that morning. "First you go off on a wild-goose chase to Japan, then you go breaking and entering into somebody's house and wind up running him off the road in Black Rock Canyon. Jesus, you're in deep trouble!"

"Somebody's got to solve this thing."

"Yeah, but not you. So it was a lovers' quarrel. So he shot his boyfriend when he got hot pants for some Polack fräulein. Big fucking deal—it's just none of your business!" We entered his office and he slammed the door behind us. "Moses, get one thing straight. You're not a private eye anymore. You work for Tulip Computer Corporation and they pay you the big bucks to toe the company line. Half the gumshoes in California would give their eyeteeth to be in your shoes. So just shut up, count your stock options, and do your fucking job!"

"It was the Wiz who told me to follow up on this thing."

"The Wiz isn't even answering your calls anymore!"

"How do *you* know that?"

Shear reddened for a second. "It's part of my job," he said quietly.

"Oh, great job you've got. What's it called? Screw your buddy?"

He shrugged. "Moses, don't make me book you on this."

"Book me? Go ahead and try. No way I ran Richardson off the goddamn road. The whole thing was a setup. I'll bet the poor bastard was down there for hours with his head bashed in before the car crashed."

"Oh, come on. That's ridiculous. You're telling me somebody jumped out of that car and let it fly over a cliff. Who could drive like that?"

"Lots of people. You, me—anyone who's scared enough to try. . . . See you around, Herbie!"

I started for the door when I heard him say, "Moses, do yourself a favor on this one, huh?"

I didn't bother replying but walked straight out of his office, down the corridor, and into the waiting room, where Toto was waiting patiently on a wooden bench. "Let's go," I said.

That night I didn't go to sleep but sat down in front of the Bulb again, inserting the Blowfish disk. It wasn't "enlightenment" I was seeking now but the truth. I might have been wrong but the way I figured it there was a killer loose, a dangerous but amateurish and paranoid killer—and Rigrod may have known it before he died, because Blowfish, like the Japanese delicacy after which it was named, had good and bad parts, maybe more than one good and bad part. Buried inside the computer game was more than likely a clue to its other side, but for whom? For me? For Cassiopeia? For what?

Once again I typed Fuck Blowfish and the words Blowfish is sea moss appeared on the screen. I sipped some black coffee and typed again: Fuck sea moss. The computer replied: I do not know how to fuck a sea moss.

Who does? I wrote back.

You have a very strange sex life, said the computer. Perhaps you are lonely.

I suppose, I typed. What is a sea moss?

What is mu?

Stop playing games. I need to know the truth.

What is truth?

You're getting very banal.

I do not understand banal.

Trite, repetitious, boring.

Why do you say I am boring?

Because people are being killed and you are dealing in platitudes.

Who is being killed?

Danny Rigrod . . . Alf Richardson.

Faggots!

What are you? A sexist computer game?

Computers are not concerned with human sex. You are not very enlightened.

I sat back, exhausted. I had played several artificial-intelligence-based computer games in the last few months but this one was by far the most resourceful. It had an astonishingly complex source code, as if its programmer had anticipated every conceivable question. But I was more convinced than ever that it contained a message, perhaps everything.

I drank more coffee, pacing around the room. It was two in the morning. The same wind I felt earlier at Richardson's place, almost a Southern California Santa Ana, was howling through the redwoods outside and shaking the windows of my house. I could feel a dry, desertlike draft coming through my fireplace. Despite its warmth, it made me shiver.

I walked over to the guest bedroom. The bed was unmade where Simon had slept and I could still see the impression of his childish form on the mattress. Out of some fatherly instinct,

I pulled up the covers when I heard a sharp, crackling noise coming from outside. I looked up to see a shadow darting past the window like one of the deer that I saw periodically racing through the night near my house, illuminated by the exterior floodlights. Perhaps the wind had scared them. Or perhaps . . .

I took a couple of steps past the bed and pulled down the blinds in the room. I walked out, shutting the door behind me, the nasty innuendos of my ex-wife—broad hints that my career endangered my children's lives and that therefore I shouldn't have them with me—flashing through my mind. To be on the safe side, I ordered Toto on alert mode and removed my revolver from the desk drawer, carrying it with me to the front door of the house. I unlocked the door and pushed it open a crack, peering outside. No one was there. I opened the door farther and took a few quiet steps out onto the front porch. Out in the darkness, maybe about fifty yards off, I could see a doe and a fawn standing by a toolshed. They stared at me for a split second, then darted off, terrified, into the woods.

Relieved, I walked back into the house and stared at the computer. Then I remembered something—*The Hagakure*—Rigrod's Bible. Given the Zen content of his computer game, perhaps it contained the clue that would unlock the mystery—my enlightenment. It had been in my briefcase since my return from Japan and I retrieved it immediately, starting to thumb through it. "Every Human Being Has Much to Learn," it said. "Hardship Is Cause for Rejoicing." "Do Everything as Though to the Death." "Artistic Accomplishments Lead to Personal Ruin." I kept going. Nothing connected. Outside, the wind had grown more intense, shaking my windows violently as if multiple pairs of giant hands were banging insistently on the panes. If someone was indeed out there, I could never hear him now.

I put the gun next to the computer and continued reading. "Choose Your Words Carefully." "Be Especially Humble After the Age of Thirty." And then: "Fish Do Not Live in Clear Water." I stopped immediately and read the section. It was a metaphorical discussion of life's complexity. Those who preached austerity were misled. All was not as it seemed. One must not overlook details and pay close attention to the obscure in order to survive. It is *the seaweed that provides fish with a hiding place in which to grow safely to maturity.* Now, what the hell did that mean?

Do blowfish hide in the sea moss? I typed into the computer.

Blowfish is sea moss.

Don't you have any other advice? I've been reading ``The Hagakure'' for half an hour and have not been able to find anything.

If you have been reading ``The Hagak- ure,'' you are on the road to wisdom.

Thanks. But I don't have much time.

The road to wisdom is not . . . But then the machine stopped, as if it were reconsidering its response. Finally it typed: Who are you?

Moses Wine.

Prove it, the machine replied.

Fine. What do you want? My mother's maiden name?

Too easy. The machine stopped again, combing through its files. I could hear the disk moving back and forth across the sectors, then stop: Who was the first to say ``Never trust anyone over thirty!'' and where did he say it?

What was this—a trivia contest? I typed Jack Weinberg in a car surrounded by the Berkeley Riot Squad in front of Sproul Hall, University of California, May 1964.

Correct.

A full-color graphic of the yin-yang symbol appeared on the screen above the words Hello, Moses. Glad to meet you.

I had made a friend.

Hello, I typed. Glad to meet you too.

Thank you. Would you like a recorded analysis of your strengths and weaknesses?

I hesitated a second. Sure.

Your strengths are a good mind and a good heart. Your weakness is nostalgia for the past, which often makes you counterproductive. What is important is to make each era as good as it can be according to its nature. The error of people who are always nostalgic for the old ways lies in their failure to grasp this point. On the other hand, people who value only what is up to date and detest anything old-fashioned are superficial.

Agreed. Who killed you?

Nobody killed me. Machines are not alive. Not even in ''2001_A Space Odyssey.''

Then who killed Danny Rigrod?

How could I know? Danny made me.

Did he finish you?

The computer did not reply instantly. Outside the wind had suddenly subsided, as if we were in the eye of a hurricane. I heard a crunching noise, like feet running across gravel. The deer again? I glanced over at Toto, whose audio-receiver system had placed him on alert. His lights were flashing and his pincer was raised above his head. I grasped the gun handle in my right hand and repeated my question to the machine with my left.

182

Did he finish you?

Your question is being processed.

Well, process fast. There may be an emergency here.

Several parts of me have been finished. Several parts are incomplete.

What parts are finished?

The same.

What parts are incomplete?

The sea moss.

The sea moss???

It is only necessary to type one?.

The sea moss?

This requires a background in computer science beyond your level. According to my stored history, your technical knowledge is approximately 6 on a scale of 100.

Give me a hint.

You will never achieve satori through hints.

I don't need satori. This is a . . .

BDOS system error. Incomplete statement.

System error? Jesus fucking Christ! Here I was in a little house in the woods all alone with an unreliable first-generation robot while some maniac possibly lurked out in the darkness and this machine was giving me system errors. I was so frustrated I was about to pick up my gun and shoot the goddamn thing, when someone beat me to it. A bullet came crashing through my living room window, spewing glass all over the floor and furniture. I dove immediately to the floor, crawled to the phone, and lifted the receiver. The line had been cut.

I turned out the house lights, took a couple of breaths to steady myself, and removed a sliver of glass from my right elbow. Then I maneuvered my body back toward the window, keeping my head just below the ledge. Clutching the revolver in my hand, I peered out quickly. I couldn't see who was holding it, but outside, protruding from a tree about fifty feet beyond my house, was the clear outline of a high-powered rifle with a telescopic sight. A split second later there was an instant retort, a bullet whistling within inches of my head. The fucker must have had an infrared sight.

I glanced behind me. Toto had become activated and was advancing clumsily in my defense. A siren wailed as the robot bounced and rolled toward the front door, blindly moving its pincer back and forth like some pathetic mine sweeper. Momentarily, another bullet rocketed through the broken window straight at Toto, smashing one of its eyes and instantly short-circuiting the robot, which toppled over on its back smoking. The pincer, disengaged, rolled free on the floor beside it while emitting a sharp, acrid smell. In my mind, I could hear Simon crying out as if his pet had been shot. The dirty motherfucker, I thought, killing an innocent robot.

Before anything else could happen, I crawled over to the computer, which fortunately was just out of sight line of the window. Keeping my gun cocked on the door, I typed on the keyboard. Help, please. Am under attack by killer with telescopic rifle.

A machine cannot help you came the reply. It is only a tool. In the search for enlightenment one can only help oneself.

I groaned, silently cursing every Japanese monk or Western disciple who ever involved himself in this narcissistic navel contemplation, when I was interrupted by the sound of feet racing across gravel. It was followed immediately by another volley of shots, smashing into a floor lamp and sending it careening against the wall, knocking down a pair of prints and a vase of eucalyptus leaves in the process. Then another bullet flashed through the side of the house. I fired back blindly, hoping to keep the intruder at bay. There was a confidence about him that was awesome, almost terrifying. Another pair of shots whistled through the front door, blasting off the bottom hinge and leaving it hanging precariously. I heard a heavy pair of boots clomping on the front porch. I fired as quickly as possible, emptying my revolver in the direction of the noise, but striking nothing, I knew. A soft laugh came from outside, but this time it was off to the side. It was as if I were being attacked by two assailants, not one.

Desperate, I turned to the computer.

Who is Cassiopeia? I typed.

There was a loud whir followed by a piercing beep I had never heard before. Eddie Capshaw came the response.

Why?

There are no why's. There is only a what.
What?

Former CIA operative assigned to infil-
trate high-tech industries and manipulate
them for intelligence and defense
purposes.

Another bullet ricocheted through the room, blasting an arm off the beleaguered cactus.

Does he understand sea moss?
He has it.

"This is it, Wine. Come on out with your hands up. And throw that little cap pistol of yours in front of you." It was Capshaw.

"Just a minute, Eddie. I'll be right there."

"You got the count of five."

What are his strengths and weaknesses?
Technologically brilliant, physically
strong. He has no weaknesses.

Oh, fuck, I thought as a last shot lashed into the door, finally blowing it off its hinges. I heard Capshaw kick it aside with his boot. "Okay, *Mr. Spade*. Five's up . . . on the hex code, the ASCI code, or any other code your puny, retarded mind cares to choose!"

The long shaft of a 40-40 assault rifle slid through the empty entranceway. I looked from it to the empty revolver in my hand. Behind me, the computer continued to whir. I glanced back to see that it was still printing out data:

```
When your opponent has no weakness,
follow the ``Book of Water.'' Strike out
with the ``all-encompassing cut.'' Be of
``munen muso''_``no mind''_and attack in a
single movement, hit him everywhere_``shuko
no mi''_with the body of the short-armed
monkey.
```

The body of the short-armed monkey? Capshaw had stepped into the room, his tall, athletic body peering down at me from the end of the rifle sight, and all I had to defend myself was more of this computerized Zen drivel.

He motioned toward my pistol. "I know it's empty—but drop it."

I tossed the pistol on the floor, letting it skitter toward the cactus plant. Capshaw backed a few steps and surveyed the area, kicking the remnants of Toto aside with his boot.

"So, Wine, around the world and back, playing in a bigger ballpark than the usual private eye."

"You might say, Eddie. Of course, you're playing in a bigger ballpark than the usual computer nerd yourself—though you never were a mere programmer."

"I know my duty."

"I thought the CIA cut you out."

"Fools." He kept the rifle on me, not letting it waver. "They all punked out. Rigrod, them. They'd rather we be invaded by a nation of techno-barbarians." He laughed softly. "But it doesn't matter. I have it all in place now."

"Have what in place? Blowfish?"

"You know, Wine, this country was founded on free enterprise, giving each man his just desserts according to his efforts. Do you think it's fair that the Russians steal the fruits of our labor, the very best products of our finest minds, simply by ripping out the insides of a game of Donkey Kong so they can stick it in their jet planes and missile-launching satellites? Sit down, Wine." I hesitated for a second and he waved the rifle at me. "Sit down!" he barked.

I retreated to the straight-backed chair near the sofa.

"You know about Russia," he continued. "They're a paranoid people, surrounded on all sides by more countries than any other nation. They'll never trust anybody. My father told me that. He knew. He was there during the war. Neither will the Japanese. They're both paranoid. Fortress states. Look at their histories—the Japanese in China, Manchuria, Burma. They may be disarmed now, but don't be misled. As we speak"—he leaned in—"secretly, somewhere, they're building underground missile installations of unbelievable sophistication. Do you think for a moment they'd be content with a paltry economic invasion? What does that mean compared to the Bushido code? Kamikaze torpedoes attacking American ships? Nothing but a display of weakness. Ha! And the Russians—they're in Afghanistan, Cuba, Finland, all over Eastern Europe on a moment's provocation. We'd be crazy to trust them. That's what my father said—trust of the barbarian leads to disaster. I mean, who stopped Attila, right? Some mealy-mouthed liberal preaching love and abnegation? That was what he said—'Who stopped Attila?'"

"Who was your father?"

"A great man totally misused and misunderstood." Capshaw advanced toward me, putting the rifle within inches of my face. "Do you understand . . . can you conceive of the disgrace of a chaplain being court-martialed? Just because he says the Devil exists in the military. If he exists in the real world, he exists in the military too! Besides, we all know the Devil is a metaphor, a metaphor for the misuse of power. Just as technology is a metaphor for man acting as God! And I want to be on God's side, don't you, Wine?"

"I don't know," I said. "I suppose so." I stared up the barrel of the rifle, past the open rear sight and the scope mount, at Capshaw's anxious blue eyes, which danced with the filmy glow of madness.

"You *suppose* so? You're an equivocator—just like Rigrod, just like Richardson! Don't you understand? Man is God. Technology is man's greatest work. We are one with technology and one with God. Fusion leads to confusion leads to the truth. Power comes out of the circuits of a microchip. And *you* stand in the way of its promulgation and *you* have to die!"

He edged his finger toward the trigger. This was it. I slammed into Capshaw's midsection, spinning past him and diving onto the floor, grabbing frantically for Toto's severed claw—"the body of the short-armed monkey."

I jumped up as Capshaw spun around, aiming the rifle at my chest. I bobbed to my right as he fired, feeling something slamming into me somewhere but paying no attention. Strike with the all-encompassing blow, I thought. Be of no mind. Hit him everywhere.

Before Capshaw could aim again, I swung the claw, hitting him first in the jaw, then in the stomach, arms, legs, groin. I was like a man possessed, a samurai in full cry. My adversary staggered backward. I continued to hit him, attacking in a single movement, whirling like a human battering ram. Face, chest, groin, and face again. Finally his head went slack. His shoulders dipped. The rifle fell to the floor. "Do what you want," he gasped. "Kill me. Anything. It's too late. Blowfish lives!" And then he hunched up, crumpling over in slow motion, the remains of his body collapsing on the floor in front of me, a bloody pulp like his mother's afterbirth.

As if instinctually, I walked to the computer and typed:

`I have Killed Capshaw.`

`Congratulations` it replied. `The game is over.`
`You have reached satori.`

Wonderful, I thought. It felt terrific. Total serenity.

And then, preprogrammed, the game started to erase itself
as I reached down and clutched my bloody side.

16

IT WAS ONLY A FLESH WOUND, but they said they wouldn't let
me out of the hospital for four days. I lay there like a lump in
semi-private at Santa Clara Valley, complaining to the nurses
and spewing back issues of the *San Jose Messenger* across the
floor like so many used-up racetrack tickets. In short, I was a
lousy patient. And I didn't even feel sick, except when I rolled
over on my side, hitting my right rib cage at a certain excru-
ciating angle. I would groan and the old man recovering from
a tracheotomy in the next bed would cackle in the most peculiar mechanical manner, straight through his artificial voice
box.

The only visitors I had in the first two days were Shear, who
arrived with a box of Toblerone chocolates and a stenographer
to record some final details of the demise of Eddie Capshaw,
and Sharon, my trusty area associate, who brought a bouquet
of native California wildflowers and a box of brioche from the

Tulip cafeteria. She also was a font of nonstop company gossip, most of which went right by me in the narcotized haze of the thirty milligrams of codeine I had been administered as a pain-killer about a half hour before. One piece of information, however, cut right through the buzz:

"They say your friend Sara and the Wiz are getting married."

"They say what?"

"You know—tying the knot, getting hitched."

"Jesus . . . " I shook my head and reached for one of the brioche by way of compensation. "That was quick."

Sharon shrugged. "Hey, my parents got married in three days when my dad was on leave from the Korean War and it's lasted thirty-seven years. Everybody I know who lived together for two years first ended up getting a divorce in six weeks."

"Uh-huh," I said. I was still digesting the information. "What else is new? Stock up?"

"Yeah, a little, but everybody's worried."

"About what?"

"Some problem on the Bulb assembly line. One of the suppliers is late with his delivery and it's balling everything up."

"What're they gonna do? Lay off the robots? Maybe they should unionize . . . affiliate with the United Metalworkers."

"Very funny, Moses."

"Yeah, I'd laugh too, only every time I do I get this sharp pain right above my middle rib. . . . So what's balling up the works?"

"Oh, one of the suppliers is late with a chip."

"What chip?"

"You think anybody tells me? I'm only an area associate."

"Plus ça change, plus c'est la même chose."

"What's that supposed to mean?"

"It's French for they fuck you either way."

"You're such a cynic, Moses."

"Yeah," I acknowledged. And I felt sad.

"Well, I'll see ya," she said, leaning over and kissing me on the cheek, trying to look cheery, like a good Silicon Valley Girl.

That night I had another visitor. It was Sara. She arrived ten minutes before the end of visiting hours in order, I imagined, to beat a hasty retreat if things got tense. She held a single red rose in her hand in a tall, crystal vase which she deposited on my bed table.

"I'm sorry," she said.

"What for?" I replied, trying to sound gallant, but it came out a little strained. "I understand congratulations are in order."

"Uh . . . yuh . . . uh-huh."

"He's a helluva guy—a legend in his time."

"He thinks very highly of you, too."

"Then how come he doesn't answer my calls?"

"I think he's embarrassed, Moses . . . about what happened."

"I don't blame him. It's like he sent me to Japan so he could steal my girl friend."

Sara reddened. "It didn't happen that way at all. I—"

"You don't have to explain." She looked relieved.

There was a moment of silence between us.

"Oh, by the way," I said, breaking it finally. "Something sad—Toto got killed. That craze-o Capshaw shot him."

"Really?" Her look of relief turned to one of concern.

"But he saved my life," I continued, half smiling. "I used his dismembered claw to kill the bastard. The broken parts are still up in my house. I know it sounds weird, but I've been lying here thinking I owe the poor robot a proper burial."

"Oh, Moses. . . ." She reached out and touched my hand. I could see she was fighting back tears. "I'll have Alex call you."

She was the first person I could remember using Wiz's real name.

"Ah, don't bother," I said. "I'll talk to him in a few days. I hear he's got bigger fish to fry at the moment."

"The Bulb assembly line?"

I nodded. "Sharon told me."

Sara shook her head.

"Bad, huh?"

"Well, it was going to be, but everything turned out all right in the end."

"What do you mean?"

"Production was going to be down two months at least. The distributors would've gone crazy. Tulip's credibility would've been finished and GTI would've ended up laughing in their beer. . . . Witherspoon was already making a move to oust Alex."

"All for a missing chip?"

"The machine doesn't work without it. Conductel, one of his oldest suppliers, just reneged on their contract."

"That's strange. What happened? Weren't they up to the technology?"

"No. It's already in all the prototypes . . . the speech chip. Fortunately, this new company named, um, Micro Memories promised to deliver the identical item within ten working days. Saved our asses." She grinned. "But I mean, after all, it's no biggie—just a 15-nanosecond, 1K CMOS."

"Sea moss?" I sat up straight in the bed as if someone had just hit me with a cattle prod.

Sara burst out laughing. "Moses, you *are* the most computer-illiterate person in the entire Silicon Valley. . . . Not *sea moss*—CMOS. . . . Complementary Metal Oxide Semiconductor—the lowest power-consuming chip available for random-access memory."

"Let's get out of here," I said, stripping off my hospital gown and climbing out of bed. "We gotta go see the Wiz!"

"Moses, you haven't been released!"

"Fuck that," I replied, reaching into the closet for my jeans and pulling them on. "Blowfish is sea moss!"

"What?"

Before she could stop me I took her arm and started leading her out of the hospital.

"I hope you know what you're doing," she said.

I didn't bother to reply.

We hardly spoke as Sara drove me in her Alfa through the back streets of what passes for downtown Sunnyvale. Although I had never been there, I had a strange premonition of where we were going as we turned between a Wells Fargo Bank and a Taco Bell, heading through the parking lot of an industrial park. It looked only about fifteen years old but there was already a sense of decay about it, the stucco flaking, a few isolated graffiti dotting the water-stained walls as if some Chicano street gangs had gotten lost on the way to the barrio and decided to leave their mark anyway, here in the middle of gringoland. A line of garages ran alongside the lot, all of them shut for the night with large corrugated-steel doors; but as we slowed, I could see light pouring through the bottom of the last one on the right end. I knew instantly it was *the garage*, the place where it all began, the Silicon Valley's very own log cabin, its Dome of the Rock, its Bodhi Tree.

We parked directly in front of it and I followed Sara up to the door. "It's me, sweetheart," she said, knocking. "I'm with Moses."

There was a twenty-second silence that felt like an hour before I heard a lock turn and watched as the door swung open, revealing an electronics lab as primitive in its way as you would have imagined Edison's, random wires spewing out of half-completed computers, microchips scattered like loose change on worktables, old posters for rock concerts on the wall that predated any, I knew, that Wiz could have possibly attended.

The man himself stood in front of me in a vintage Hawaiian shirt, staring down at the concrete of the garage floor as if he were doing penance. Then, suddenly, he stared up at me, a ferocious anger overtaking his depression.

"You bastard," he said. "Why'd you force her to bring you here? Don't you have any idea how embarrassing this is for her?"

Not the slightest hint of a stammer. I was reminded of a theory I had read years before of stuttering being a mask for unacknowledged aggression.

"I didn't have a choice, Wiz," I replied flatly, staring him straight in the eyes. He faced down again.

"W-wha do you mean?" he said.

"Blowfish is sea moss . . . or, as you say, CMOS."

Wiz took a step backward as if I had hit him. "H-how do you know?" he said.

"It was a clue in Rigrod's little computer game. My guess is he knew he was treading in dangerous waters and wanted to leave a message in a bottle. Who's Micro Memories, Wiz?"

"I-I don't know. I-I sorta just heard of them this week." He looked over nervously at Sara. She smiled at him reassuringly, came over, and put her arm around him. I felt a twinge of jealousy.

"They just called you up out of nowhere, huh? Made you an offer you couldn't refuse?" He didn't respond. "Why don't we start from the beginning?" I said. "Why'd you hire me?"

"G-guilt."

"That's what I figured. You know what they say about guilt, don't you? When you're guilty, it means you want to do it again."

"D-don't be cruel, Moses."

"Okay, okay. So you hired me because you were guilty. Guilty about what? Black Widow, I imagine."

Wiz nodded. I glanced over at Sara, who had wrapped both her arms around his waist, cradling him like a son. "L-last year, when we were r-really in trouble, al-almost going under . . . w-when I was about to lose control of the c-company . . . some p-people came to me, w-wanted to make a big in-investment, provide us with all the capital we n-needed."

"As long as you didn't ask any questions. And I suppose they wanted to pick their own personnel as well—Rigrod, Capshaw, Laura Suzuki. So you went along with these 'people,' but then you felt bad about it and—"

"H-hired you to catch me." He looked away again, staring at the walls of his garage with a pained expression on his face. In the corner of the room I could see a cot with the sheets thrown back where he must have been sleeping. A frayed poster for the first Tulip Ii was tacked to the Sheetrock above the pillow, next to an autographed picture of John and Yoko. "You know, Moses, i-in this country you can dream all you w-want, but w-we're all working for the government or G-GTI in the end."

I knew what he meant. In some ways it sounded like a weak excuse, but there was too much truth in it to contradict. It seemed beside the point to state the obvious—that in other societies you didn't even have the option of serving the corporation. Wiz had eaten the Forbidden Fruit and that was that. "Yeah, well," I said. "Rigrod clearly didn't feel too good about it either. That's why Capshaw let him have it, but not too soon to destroy Blowfish. Your Black Widow's little offspring. . . . Any idea what it is?"

He shook his head. "We m-make personal computers," he added lamely.

"Uh-huh. What about the chip from Micro Memories? Do you have one?"

He looked at me a moment, then walked over to one of the worktables, pointing at one of several chips that were lying in no particular order next to what I recognized as the mother board of a Bulb computer. I stepped closer for a better look at it. To me it looked like every other microchip I had seen, a black centipede accidentally flipped on its back with its hundred metal legs pointing catatonically upward.

"CMOS is actually the updating of an old technology," said Sara, trying to sound matter-of-fact. "In the fifties and sixties they called them field-effect transistors."

"Have you tried it?" I said to Wiz, nodding toward the mother board.

"Of c-course. It works."

"It governs the Bulb's speech capability, doesn't it?" I half smiled. "Like Toto."

"A-among others th-things. Every chip has many u-uses."

"Right." I started to pick it up, but then realized I might contaminate it. "Look," I said, "it's pretty clear why Rigrod called it Blowfish. For him, Japanese culture had all the answers, and blowfish is a type of sashimi that is said to be exquisite if properly prepared, but can kill you almost instantly if you eat the wrong parts. I imagine this chip is some kind of blowfish."

Wiz folded his arms in front of him, clutching his opposite shoulders as if to ward off a blow. Sara came up behind him and held him gently around the chest. They waited for me to continue.

"You see, nobody knew what Blowfish was—not the Russians from their listening point up at the consulate, or the shady Japanese businessmen who had exploited poor Laura Suzuki all those years. They only knew it was something important, something smart. The only ones who *really* knew were Rigrod and Capshaw . . . besides those 'people' of yours who hired them. Hence they invented the game as a distraction, a cover for what they were really doing that could fool Laura, Maximov, even, thankfully, Capshaw himself once Rigrod realized the folly." I shook my head. "He must've been one twisted, brilliant motherfucker. . . . Ever read *The Hagakure*?"

"What's that?" asked Sara.

"Some eighteenth-century samurai tome Rigrod swore by. It advocates homosexual love, silence, and embracing death. . . . But that leaves us with the real Blowfish. You see, my guess is it was meant to be stolen."

Sara and Wiz looked at each other.

"Not in the usual way," I continued, "or for the usual reasons. But accidentally. Remember, it wasn't too long ago that Nicky Li got knocked off in the restaurant in Chinatown. That was no accident. When I arrived at his former headquarters in the Akihabara in Tokyo, Maximov—the Russian section chief from good old San Francisco—was already waiting for me. *And* they—Nicky's old company under its new management—already claimed to be preparing a counterfeit Bulb computer, just as they had previously ripped off the Ii and, I assume, the GTI PC and any other product they thought they could make a buck on in the international market. No big deal, normally, but think again. What happens to those computers and what're guys like Maximov doing in Akihabara?"

"B-buying them and t-taking them to the Soviet Union."

"Right. And for what? So some Moscow high school kid can lust over Ms. Pac-Man in the privacy of his own home? No way. They take them, break them up, and use the microchips in the guidance systems of every air, sea, or land weapon they've got. We know that. They are—as Capshaw said—a land of paranoid techno-barbarians. And Capshaw knew damn well precisely what was inside Blowfish. Unfortunately, I think the next ones to know are going to be the people operating those Russian weapons—or maybe even the poor sucker piloting an Aeroflot jet from Gorki to Irkutsk—after those eager slobs get their hands on their first Bulb computers complete with the new razzle-dazzle CMOS chip from Micro Memories. . . . Hell, the boys at Micro Memories don't even know what's programmed into it themselves, do they? They just copied the plans. I wonder where they got those."

Wiz looked grim. He leaned against the worktable and shut his eyes.

"I know it sounds weird, but it's the only way I could make sense of this thing. That's what a blowfish does—it tastes great but it kills you if you take it the wrong way."

"Y-you m-mean," said Wiz, his eyes opening only slightly, "we're *trying* to plant our ch-chips in their weapons. . . ."

"Trick them into taking it. Look . . . if we've known for years they've been using our chips, stealing them from everywhere—kids' toys, stereos, *computers*—why *wouldn't* we make one that was a plant . . . booby-trap one to blow up in their faces—a blowfish! Besides, since they can't understand how to make chips as advanced as ours, they'd never know what hit them. We could do anything we wanted. They'd be almost powerless to stop it!"

"Oh, come on, Moses," said Sara. "This is ridiculous. If Alex believed you, he'd have to cancel the order, stop the assembly line for God knows how long, sink Tulip and himself along with it. A lot of people work for this company, not to mention believe in what it stands for—things *you,* of all people, are supposed to support and respect! That is, unless you've been a hypocrite all your life!"

Wiz interrupted before I could reply. "Let's t-test it," he said.

He picked up the CMOS with a pair of tweezers and slid it into the mother board. Then he snapped the board back into the computer and turned it on. The Tulip logo booted up instantly.

"Now what?" said Sara, unable to disguise her impatience.

"Talk to it," I said.

"Hello, Baker-Charlie, testing—one, two, three." The words spilled out almost instantaneously on the Bulb screen.

"See," she said. "Normal. Now get out of here, Moses, and leave us in peace." She stared at me with a look of tremendous intensity, a tigress protecting her man. For a moment I hesitated.

"Just one thing, Sara." I turned away and leaned over the machine. "*Dasvidanya, tovarisch*"—Good-bye, comrade—I said, speaking the only words of Russian I knew other than *nyet* and *vodka*. Nothing happened.

"Okay, that's enough," said Sara. She reached for the back of the machine to turn it off, but Wiz intercepted her.

"T-to activate voice r-recognition, you must speak with a p-proper accent. Otherwise the c-curve doesn't match." He looked at the machine and pronounced two words in a crisp, unstuttering Russian: "*Brosai bombu!*" They appeared on the screen as quickly as the English had.

"What's that mean?" I asked.

"D-drop the bomb," said Wiz flatly, not allowing the slightest hint of a smile to betray the irony of his choice. The words faded off the screen in a couple of seconds, just as the English had, and Sara laughed, relieved that again nothing had happened. This particular CMOS was no more than it was intended to be—certainly not a macabre, high-tech implant to foul the advanced weapons systems of enemy powers, a life-endangering device as sinister in its way as germ warfare because no one could predict where the little item would end up or how those techno-barbarians would use it. They didn't even have to put it in a weapon. The naive idiots could put the chip in the control room of the Moscow subway, for crissakes, or the processing center of a major city hospital or the fuel injection of any public bus and drive themselves off the goddamn road—all the time thinking they had co-opted the most advanced American technology!

Anyway, it seemed as if I had been wrong. The computer screen was blank and all appeared well. But then I stared at the Wiz. He seemed to have come to a different conclusion. He couldn't take his eyes off the machine. His expression was ashen. A single tear started to roll down his right cheek. I smelled the air. There was a strange bitterness, like something burning—rubber or wire or maybe both. A short circuit. Sara gripped Wiz's shoulder. Suddenly smoke appeared, spurting out of the vents in the back of the computer. Then came sparks, spewing out like Fourth of July fireworks running on their side. I reached to turn the machine off, but this time Wiz stopped me, restraining my arm with a force I had no idea he had. "No! Let it go!" he shouted. "Let it *all* go!"

He jumped up and ran to a closet, grabbed a can of lighter fluid, and squirted it in the direction of the worktable.

"Jesus, Alex, what're you doing?" Sara screamed.

"It's already ashes as far as I'm concerned. The whole fucking thing. They can have it! C'mon." He grabbed both our hands and started leading us out of the garage, slamming the door shut behind him. "Don't worry. The walls are fireproof. . . . I just couldn't bear to see this place ever again!"

He was right. We stood there silently for the next half hour watching the interior fire through the garage window and hearing the mini-explosions when the flames ate through the furniture and the computers to the cathode-ray tubes. It was quite a display, really—not as sad as I would have expected.

When it was over, Wiz turned to his woman. "I want to go now, Sara. I want to go to some far part of the world where no one knows us, like Kashmir, and just be there for a long time with you. You want to come?"

She answered him with a deep, loving hug.

"Good-bye, Moses." He shook my hand warmly. "It's been a pleasure knowing you."

"Good-bye, Alex," I said. "I certainly feel the same way. I'm sure I'll be quitting Tulip immediately too . . . I think I was born for the corporate life even less than you were."

"I know," he said.

Then he walked over to a pay phone and, as his last act as head of the Tulip Computer Corporation, sent a telegram to Micro Memories canceling the order for the CMOS chips—although we all knew it was fruitless. Once a monster like that was created, there was almost nothing you could do to prevent it from running amok. It would turn up—an innocent add-on—in somebody else's computer or video tape deck.

Wiz acknowledged that with a sad smile and we got into Sara's car and started back into the hills. The last I saw of them was twenty minutes later, when they dropped me off at my house and drove off with a friendly honk into the darkness—not stopping, I imagined, until they reached Kashmir.

As for me, I woke up early the next morning and buried a robot. Then I got into my car and started heading back to L.A. to see my kids. No, corporate life was not for me. I thought, once again as I drove, of more of those strange words of wisdom from Rigrod's *Hagakure*. At that moment, compared to many of them, these made the most sense to me:

> Human life lasts but an instant. One should spend it doing what one pleases. In this world fleeting as a dream, to live in misery doing only what one dislikes is foolishness!